THE WHITE ROOM

The White Room

by ELIZABETH COATSWORTH

Illustrated by George W. Thompson

PANTHEON BOOKS

1

$\mathcal{H}$IGH FARM was notable for two things: beauty and loneliness. But the man in the doorway of the great barn—a landmark for miles around—had at the moment no eye for beauty, and paid little attention to loneliness either. Gus Treadwell was perhaps in his forties, strongly built, ruddy, with eyelids drawn straight down to the outer corners of half-hidden blue eyes. He had a bluff and hearty look, and quite possibly a temper, as well. For the rest, his most remarkable feature was his sandy hair.

From where he stood, he could see north, west, and south, across snowy fields to a landscape of hills which ringed the farm on three sides: the Camdens, Haystack, the Raggeds, the China Hills, and so to the White Mountains, where, far off, Mt. Washington raised its inch of splendor, bright in distant sunshine. But these were for the present no concern of his. He was trying to decide whether or not there would be more snow. The hilltop winds had swept some of the pasture bare in the steep south fields, the day was warmer, and Gus was considering putting the sheep out for exercise and air. They worried him. Several of them were acting sick. When he spoke of it at breakfast, his wife, Laura, suggested sending for the veterinarian, but as often happened, her advice, perhaps because of the uncertainty in her voice, turned him balky.

"Vets cost money," he said, "and Jim Clark don't know any more about sheep than I do. I can doctor them all right without anyone's help."

Laura didn't say anything more. But Maidie, his older sister, who sat next to him at table, remarked, "All they need is a mite of fresh air."

There was nothing uncertain in Maidie's voice. Maidie had a lot of common sense. She was nearly ten years older than Gus, and it was she, more than his own mother, who had raised him. She'd given up her life to him, and he was grateful and showed it. One of the things which troubled him was her health. Somehow it made him feel guilty that ever since coming to High Farm she had complained a lot about her backaches and headaches. It was for his sake that she stayed on in a place that didn't agree with her. She was the most unselfish woman in the world, and it hurt her to leave all the work for Laura to do. Time and time again she tried to help, but it always brought on one of her spells and she'd have to quit. Yet there she'd sit, cheerful and sweet, between the stove and the window, with the morning sun lighting her up, bright as a dollar, her eye on everything, and a word of good advice always ready. He didn't know what he'd do without Maidie.

Even with her advice, things hadn't gone too well, as Gus admitted sometimes to himself in the dark and early hours of the morning when he couldn't sleep. High Farm had been famous in the county when he married Laura King and took over its management. The hayfields then were cut clean to the walls; there were barley and rye fields, too, and a first-rate herd of registered cattle. Everything was in good order inside and out. House and barn equipment were of the best. He had been so proud of the place! And now? And now? When these thoughts came to Gus in his sleepless bed he turned and twisted, turned and twisted.

"It's not my fault," he told himself angrily. "Prices keep going up and down. After old Tom died, I had to do it myself or run worse into debt. I'd worked along with him for over a year, and as Maidie said, a man can learn all he needs to know about farming in a year. Laura wanted me to get someone to help like her father used to have. She doesn't say anything, but when she looks around, she must think I'm not much good. I'll prove to her yet that I can keep the farm up like it used to be. But these days it's out of the question to get help with wages what they are. And with three children coming along, what do you expect? I can't be blamed for not keeping up the fields. Just now the only thing I can do is to let the land go to blueberries, and sell the crop on the bush. Maidie says so, too. And sheep are a lot easier to take care of than cows—or at least so I was told. But Joe Duncan certainly took advantage of me when he sold me this lot. First it's been one thing and then it's another. If I keep on losing them—"

Now, looking at the sky, Gus couldn't make up his mind what the weather would do. The tarnished cow weathervane pointed into the northwest, and that should mean clearing. But as he walked round the corner of the barn followed by Rex, the old collie, he was met with flurries of wind blowing from the east. Under a show of blue sky lay a heavy white band of cloud, a "snowbank" as people called it at this time of the year. Below the snowbank flashed the sea along the whole eastern horizon, its silver broken only by the flecks of two or three islands. But, worried and uncertain, Gus saw neither sea nor islands.

Still with his mind not made up, Gus tramped back into the barn. In their pen, the sheep turned to watch him. Half a dozen were lying with their heads stretched out in the straw. He stood staring at them a long time, filled with pity and uncertainty. He didn't like their look. Should he send for Jim Clark after all? It might be nothing important, and that would mean more good money down the drain.

Outside the wind was rising, and once again it was whispering and rubbing against the buildings and sending shallow rivers of loose snow flowing down the slopes. The house was built of gray stone, quarried from the rock on which it stood. No wind could shake it. The great barn had been raised by men trained in shipbuilding. It was ribbed and raftered with oak beams and stood foursquare as when it was built. The shed, which connected the two, was a later addition, put up by Laura's grandfather, and here the windows shook a little in the gusts and snow sifted under the outer door. But that was all. Only outdoors could the wind manifest its power. It dwarfed and bent the apple trees. The bark of the lilac bush by the front door was twisted as though wrung between two powerful hands. The paired elm trees, planted when the house was built, grew small and brittle. Only where High Hill plunged steeply down to the valley, the beechwoods in the shelter of the south cliff grew to their proper shape.

Here on the hilltop it was impossible to escape the wind. As Maidie complained, no flowers flourished. Here laundry was whipped off the line and smoke was torn from the chimneys. Here the sun shone brighter, the well water tasted colder, and the wind came and went like a familiar. Here if one looked about one, the eye learned a taste for distances, for far horizons, for the unknown. The real and the imagined became indistinguishable. Fact and dream walked side by side. Here Laura had been born and raised. The place was in her blood. But to Maidie, at least, it was the enemy.

The children were now at school, but they would be back before dark, when the lowlands lay in shadow but the sun still glittered in the High Farm windows. The big yellow school bus would come jolting up the lane, and while it turned its clumsy length in the dooryard the children would clatter into the shed, hang up their coats, rip off their overshoes, and hurry into the kitchen, each going straight as a filing to a magnet: Mildred to Aunt Maidie in her rocking chair; Paul upstairs to his room, two steps at a time, to make sure that his rabbit was safe in its box; Alvinia, the youngest, to find her father.

"Daddy! Daddy!" she shouted if she didn't see him at once. "Daddy! Where are you?"

But now the house was empty of children. When Gus came in from the barn, followed by Rex, he found Maidie in her usual place reading yesterday's newspaper. As always, she looked dressed for company, and her hair, sandy like his own but a little faded, stood out in a neat friz about her small face. On seeing her brother she at once folded the paper and took off her glasses.

"Well, now," she asked, "what did you decide? Going to let the sheep out for a while?"

"Can't make up my mind about the weather."

"The wind's rising," said Laura, not turning from the sink shelf where she was rolling out pie crust.

"The wind's always rising here," said Maidie. "You can't pay any attention to it, Gus. Go on and let the poor creatures out. It'll do them good."

14

Without answering, Gus took the *Old Farmer's Almanac* from its nail by the stove and, thumbing over its ruffled pages, sat down on the cot which stood in the corner behind Maidie's chair.

"Here we are. December nineteenth. 'Expect more snow and freezing weather.' "

"That old farmer never gets things straight. If he says more snow, there'll likely be a thaw. Sun's trying to come out this minute."

Before Gus could answer, Laura came noiselessly to the stove, slipped the pie into the oven, added a couple of pieces of wood to those in the firebox, and, turning, walked to the shed door where she took down an old red sweater and put it on. She did not guess that Maidie's eyes were watching her, acknowledging the slow grace with which she moved.

"They wanted her to be Ceres at the grange," Maidie thought. "She'd have been a much better one than that beanpole they have now, but Gus is too tired nights to go skiting off to the grange in all weathers," and, thinking of Gus, she remembered the discussion at hand and forgot her sister-in-law, who had already gone out.

With the outer door of the shed shut behind her, Laura paused for a moment to look into the eye of the wind. Pure and clear, the air rushed upon her, whipping her cotton skirts against her legs, blowing her dark, soft hair across her face. It was too cold to stand there long, but that moment she allowed herself.

The laundry lines were stretched behind the barn,

where the wind had swept clear the dome of granite on which the farm was built. The clothes were frozen, as Laura knew they would be. They were stiff and cold as the corpses of clothes, and as she tried to detach them they fought her off, crackling and beating against her face and hands. After the clothespins had been pried loose, the clothes still gripped the line in frozen death-grasps which she had to force open one by one with ice-cold fingers, very gently for fear of tearing the brittle cloth. At last her arms were filled with the first load, rigid and flat and arctic against her living body. Even so, her eyes, as she turned back toward the house, rested on the distant mountains with brooding delight. She had forgotten about the discussion she had left in the kitchen, her mind swept clear by the fierce wind. But as she passed by the barn she heard the rumble of the big door sliding open, and remembered.

"Maidie's argued Gus into putting out the sheep," she thought.

Her husband stepped into view and slid the heavy door to behind him.

"Another one's dead," he told her.

"Oh, Gus!" she exclaimed. "I'm so sorry!"

But he turned away. If he had wanted sympathy from her when he spoke, he no longer wanted it. Or perhaps he could not take it when given.

"You've got to expect losses," he said over his shoulder. "I'll bet your dad had plenty."

2

$\mathcal{T}$IRED AS SHE WAS, Laura could not sleep. It was very cold in the unheated bedroom where she lay, although during the day a little heat came up from the kitchen below through an open register in the bedroom floor. But that died away as the fire in the stove died, and the cold crept out from every wall and window and took possession of the room. Fortunately, Laura was used to cold and did not mind it. It was not cold which now kept her awake, but hope. For at midnight a new year would be born.

As she lay looking about her, the room seemed as it had when she was a child, for the moonlight, flooding the unshaded windows, disguised the stains on wallpaper and panelling. Her parents had slept in the same mahogany bed which she and Gus now used. The mahogany bureau was gone. Maidie had taken a fancy to that for her own room, but she had not wanted the heavy chiffonier, nor the low chair by the window where Laura's mother used sometimes to sit at her darning on summer afternoons, because from there the view was even more unbroken than from downstairs.

The Kings had always made a good deal of New Year's. Living as they did, rather isolated from the rest of the world, they had developed a ritual of public holidays with a few private ones of their own. Every year, on the day when Laura found the first violet, her mother made a layer cake, and an upside-down pudding celebrated the return of the first robin. A molasses candy-pull marked the first evening of snow. Laura's memories were filled with delightful occasions. After her marriage, she had tried to keep up the old customs but had met with only indifference.

"Laura, darling," Maidie had said in her sweetest voice, "doesn't it really seem a little childish to make a fuss over a violet? You're grown up now, you know," and Gus had only halfheartedly come to her defense. Slowly the little garland of festivals withered away, until only Christmas, Easter, Fourth of July, Thanksgiving, and, to a lesser extent, New Year's managed to survive—yes, and birthdays. Every year Laura baked five birthday cakes and five times lighted candles. She baked no cake and lighted no candles for herself, and although Maidie occasionally scolded herself for having once more forgotten, no one ever made a cake for her.

But this New Year's Eve, Laura could not sleep. Things must not go on as they were going, and with the help of a new year, they need not.

"It's as much my own fault as anybody's," Laura thought, lying quietly, her hands loosely crossed on her breast. "Maidie means to be kind, I'm sure. She often speaks to me very lovingly. And of course you can't have sandy hair without having tempers. When things begin to get tense—at the very beginning—if I could only laugh the way Mamma used to, everything would be much simpler."

The clock at the foot of the stairs struck eleven slow strokes and trembled into silence.

"Next year," Laura thought, "—and that's in another hour!—I'll make a resolution not to think about the way things used to be when Papa and Mamma were alive. And I mustn't let myself wonder why no one seems to love me. I'm sure they do, especially Gus. He's embarrassed to show it in front of Maidie. I remember the time she saw him kissing me, not long after she first came here to live. She sailed out of the room as if we'd been doing something sinful. I wish he didn't pay so much attention to what she thinks! But it's foolish to get this trapped feeling. I can go right on loving all of them. And that's what matters."

She moved a little so that her shoulder just touched her husband's, taking comfort in his nearness, listening to his slow, strong breathing. So she lay, making her resolutions until the clock in the hall sounded

21

once more, a deep, soft stroke. The house was per-
fectly silent except for the very delicate sigh of the
cold wind outside.

Almost without conscious plan, Laura slipped out
of bed, put her bare feet into her old slippers, found
her wrapper on the back of a chair, and tiptoed to
the window. As she had expected, the moon was full
or almost full, but she had not expected the great
ring of light about it like the curbstone of a well, nor
the deep bottomless black inside that ring, at the
exact center of which floated the moon.

Outwards from the circle the sky was hazed over,
dulling the stars.

"The moon is wading deep in snow," Laura
thought, repeating the country saying.

It was hard to look away from the marvel, but at
last Laura's eyes sought the sea. There in a long bar
it lay, burning upwards in white fire toward the moon.

"The whales are spouting quicksilver," she thought.
She had never seen a whale, but always she imagined
them, beyond the whale-shaped islands, living their
mysterious, innocent lives, courting and frolicking,
bringing forth their young and nursing them in the
alien depths of the sea.

For a long time Laura stood in the icy room waiting
for something, she could not have said what. But
nothing happened. Only the moon in its black pit of
space stared down, and the bright unwinking sea
stared back, and the snow, with its motionless shadows, held the trance. Six weeks ago the globe of the

great earth itself had rung its hollow answer even to so small a foot as Alvinia's, but now all was softness and soundlessness. Laura loved winter, at least when she looked out at it. Nowadays the fresh snow was too beautiful and immaculate as a setting for the buildings at High Farm in their disrepair. Noble still in line and bearing, she liked them best in the rain or at dusk when their present state was softened and the past returned to them for a little while. So far the damage was on the surface and would not be too difficult to repair, but a few years more of neglect would eat into the essential fabric. Quickly she checked her thoughts. A new year, a new hope, was about to begin!

Quietly Laura turned and felt her way down the hall, testing the floor with each step for fear that some board might creak. From here the clock ticked reassuringly: "Time comes, time goes, and in the end all sorrows are forgotten." The door of the room where Maidie slept with the two girls was closed to keep in the heat. Long ago, when she first came to the farm, she had told Gus that she wanted the stove from the parlor brought upstairs.

"If I'm going to stay here" ("But it's only for a few months!" thought Laura), "at least I don't have to freeze to death."

Gus never complained of the amount of firewood Maidie used, although he often told Laura that she burned too much in the kitchen stove.

"If you had the cutting to do, you women would take more care," he would say. When he was criticiz-

ing Laura he often addressed her as "you women."
But he never said "you women" to Maidie.

The door of Paul's room stood open to catch a little
bedtime heat from downstairs. As Laura went by she
heard something stir, but it was not Paul, his lanky
young body rolled up into a ball under the quilts, his
dark, thin face drawn down, half out of sight. It was
his beloved rabbit, moving in its box.

The coming of this animal had been strange. One
morning early in December Paul had sat down to
breakfast in an unusually talkative mood. He had had
a dream about a rabbit. Not an ordinary rabbit, he
said, but a magic rabbit. It could do wonderful things.

"What?" Alvinia asked, interested and forthright.

Paul's face clouded. The dream, which had seemed
so clear, was growing vague. He couldn't remember
exactly what the dream rabbit could do, but it was
wonderful.

"Get on with your breakfast," his father interrupted. "School bus won't wait," and Paul's wonderful rabbit had been forgotten.

But that very afternoon he came running into the
kitchen in great excitement.

"Mamma, there's a rabbit in the barn, and he's
tame!"

Before Laura could say anything, a very large white
rabbit came hopping through the open shed door into
the kitchen, where it sat in the middle of the floor
looking calmly about it. It was a snowshoe hare in its
winter coat, pure white except for gray patches on the

24

tips of its ears, and, unlike a domestic white rabbit's, its eyes were dark brown. Mildred ran to pick it up, but it hopped off, taking its stand behind the stove where she couldn't reach it.

"Let him alone!" Paul said. "He doesn't like to be touched. He won't let even me pick him up."

From the first Paul took it for granted that the rabbit was his and his alone.

"But he must belong to someone," Laura said. "He's used to people."

"He belongs to me!" Paul answered almost fiercely. "I dreamed about him and then he came."

In spite of his protests, Laura telephoned to all the neighbors. No one had lost a rabbit or even knew of a tame one on High Hill.

"Wait until Mother Brindle sees him!" prophesied Maidie from her rocking chair. But when the cat came in, notable huntress that she was, she pretended not to see the newcomer, and Rex, too, at his first encounter fixed his dimming eyes upon the stranger for a long minute and then turned away.

"What's his name?" asked Alvinia, who liked things to be clear.

"I don't know yet." Paul shook his head.

But two days later, having read through half the school's copy of *Hiawatha*, he came home with a name. "He's the Wabasso."

"You can't call him 'the' something," said Mildred with an older sister's disdain.

"Yes, I can. Longfellow says 'the rabbit, the

Wabasso.' It sounds like 'Your Royal Highness' or something."

"Well, he acts like 'Your Royal Highness or something,' " said Maidie. "He's been sitting there, staring at me for ten minutes. It makes me nervous. Shoo, you silly thing!"

But the Wabasso only moved when he wanted to.

Most often with the fall of night, but occasionally at other times, he would be overtaken by moods of wildness, during which he would bound round and round the kitchen, close to the wall.

"Drat that rabbit!" Maidie then cried. "For goodness' sakes, Paul, put him upstairs before he drives me crazy."

"He'll quiet down soon," Paul would say. "There's a storm coming."

Sometimes it seemed to Laura that the rabbit sensed human storms as well, and his race round the baseboards more than once was prelude to some outbreak of Maidie's temper or Gus's irritability.

From Laura's point of view, the important thing about the Wabasso was his effect on Paul. From the moment the boy had clapped eyes on the rabbit, he wakened a little from the dream world in which he seemed to live so much of the time. His teacher, Miss McClure, said that he was taking more interest in his studies, and that he sometimes played with the other boys at recess, instead of wandering off by himself. Laura noticed the difference, too. Nowadays Paul usually heard the first time he was spoken to, and there was less friction between him and his father.

"Dear Wabasso," Laura thought gratefully, as down the stairs she went, skipping the second tread, which always groaned under any weight. At the foot of the steps she reached out for a moment to touch the smooth wood of the grandfather's clock. She felt it throb a very little under her fingers, shaken by its own ticked heartbeats. A clock knows nothing. It takes no comfort from a touch. But a lonely human being takes comfort where he can, in memories, in moonlight, in a clock which has stood in the same place for longer than anyone can remember.

The last glow had died out of the ashes in the fire-box, but Laura rebuilt the fire, pouring a little kerosene on the kindling from the tin can she kept for the purpose. At the touch of the first match the flames began their small lion roaring, and Laura adjusted the drafts before pulling the kettle over the heat.

Old Rex, who had been lying in the warmest corner of the room, walked stiffly across to her and stood looking up into her face. She leaned down and stroked his head.

"It will be midnight in less than half an hour, Rex. We're going to celebrate," she whispered. And at the sound of a voice, Mother Brindle, who had been curled up on the old cot, rose, stretched, and, leaping lightly to the floor, joined the other two.

Laura took the new almanac from its nail and sat

down in Maidie's chair. At once the cat jumped into her lap, circled briefly, and settled herself comfortably. Rex took more time, groaning a little as he lowered himself to the floor at her feet.

Always, just before midnight, Mr. King had read aloud from the New Year's page of the almanac, as now Laura did to the listening animals:

"A Flower unblown; a Book unread;
    A Tree with fruit unharvested;
    A Path untrod; a House whose rooms
    Lack yet the heart's divine perfumes;
    A Landscape whose wide border lies
    A silent shade, 'neath silent skies;
    A wondrous Fountain yet unview'd;
    A Damsel ready to be woo'd:
    This is the Year that for you waits
    Beyond to-morrow's mystic gates."

The reading finished, Laura got up, lifting Mother Brindle carefully down to the floor, and put a little coffee and a cup of hot water in the old blue pot to boil. Just as she thought, it was almost midnight, and a moment later the clock began to boom from the hallway. Smiling, she hurried to get the broom from its place in the corner and, for once flinging wide the outside door, swept the Old Year over the threshold and into the cold glare of the moonlight. Although she felt the bite of the wind on her bare ankles, she did not hurry to close the door until, having swept the Old Year out, she had bowed the New Year in.

"Do come in and make yourself at home," she murmured. "I hope you bring peace and happiness to the world, and to us," and then she added to the old ritual, speaking under her breath, "I do need help so badly!"

When she had closed and locked the door, the good odor of boiling coffee already filled the kitchen. She brought a pitcher of milk and put some in Rex's big saucer and Mother Brindle's small one. Then she poured out a cup of coffee for herself and, sitting down again in the rocking chair, sipped it slowly. The room was filled with gentle shadows and the sound of the animals as they lapped their milk while Laura enjoyed her coffee. She didn't think consciously of her parents or of the year ahead. She was caught in the solace of the moment. The little festival, held with no other companions than an old dog, a brindled cat, and a moon in a black well of space, had turned her heart toward hope.

When her cup was empty she rose and, stepping lightly, put the kitchen in order, rinsing out the pot, washing the cup, patting old Rex again, putting Mother Brindle back on the cot. Before turning out the light, she looked about her with guilty amusement. She had wasted firewood and coffee, and given the animals sweet milk when they were supposed to have only the sour leftovers. She had opened the door, which was never opened in winter because it chilled off the house. She had stayed up when she should have been asleep, and gone through a ridiculous rigmarole which showed she hadn't the sense she'd been born with, and likely as not she'd end up by coming down with a cold and dragging around for days, neglecting her work.

"Going out half naked like that!" she could hear Maidie's accusing voice.

"But you won't know a thing about it, Maidie!" she thought, almost gaily. "And now the New Year's properly at home at High Farm, probably sitting in your rocking chair at this very moment!"

Looking about once more to make sure that she had left no telltale trace of the adventure for Maidie's suspicions to latch on to in the morning, Laura turned out the light, eased open the door into the hall, slipped out, closed it, and like a ghost went up the clock-sounding stair. But as she passed the door of Maidie's room there came a dry cough from the four-post bed within. It was not the cough of a person asleep or half asleep. Maidie was wide awake and letting Laura know it.

3

On the first of January, the sun rose from the sea in triumphant brightness, and High Farm was like a beacon flashing back a welcome across the shadowy lowlands. If the moon had foretold new snow, there was no sign of it as yet, and Laura moved about the kitchen with a sense of expectancy. Gus had already put out Rex and the cat and lighted the morning fire in the stove. The kitchen was beginning to warm up as she set the table and prepared breakfast. Soon the children ran in with half their clothes on to finish dressing by the stove.

"Happy New Year!" they called. "Happy New Year!" and Maidie, last to appear, just as the oatmeal was ready to serve, said, "Happy New Year, everybody!" very cheerfully.

The general good humor lasted all through breakfast. As a treat, Laura served pancakes and syrup with slices of fried sausage meat, which Gus always liked, and there was no squabbling among the children. After breakfast Paul went out to help his father in the barn, and the girls, without protest, went upstairs to make beds. Maidie retired to her chair with her fancy knitting and did not bring up the question of what Laura had been doing the night before downstairs at such an hour, and as for Laura, she began her usual morning by clearing the table of the breakfast dishes.

From the window above the sink her glance ranged the field slopes and across twenty miles of pond, river, and headlands to the narrow strip of sea, and to all the mysteries of the sea and the ships which sailed it, and the foreign continents along its shores, which, forever invisible though they might be, were always part of Laura's awareness. Voyagers from the unknown of a different sort, birds continually materialized, their wings edged with light. The bluejays flew with a strong joyousness like boys leaping down a hillside from rock to rock, occasionally shrieking with harsh delight. The juncos were quiet birds, and the chickadees seemed to give cheerful thanks each time they pounded open a sunflower seed with a little rat-tat-tat on the board which Mr. King had on one long-ago day fastened to the sill as a feeding stand. Of all the flock, the tree sparrows were the least afraid. They made room for the bluejays, but when the big birds were gone, the small ones sometimes shared with one another and sometimes tried to hold the fort for

34

themselves with warlike peepings and small combats in the air, where two champions met beak to beak, and little claw to claw, their wings fanning mightily to keep the fighters aloft in this off-balance position.

In these duels they never seemed to hurt one another, yet there was a victor and a vanquished, and one returned to the stand, while the other watched from a twig of the nearest apple tree.

Usually Laura waited until she was alone in the kitchen before putting out the mixture of crumbs, chicken feed, and sunflower seeds which she kept in a covered bowl. More than once Maidie, watching the birds as they fed, had spoken about Laura's wastefulness. But this morning was the beginning of a new year at the farm, and, filled with resolutions to live more naturally, without always being afraid of what Maidie might think or say, Laura opened the window without a glance at her sister-in-law. Unfortunately, at the sound, a junco, which had been searching along the cracks for lost seeds, flew up and, in its confusion, lost its bearings and fluttered into the kitchen.

Instantly Maidie was on her feet.

"A bird!" she shrieked. "You've let a bird in the house! That means one of us will die inside the year!"

Before Laura could stop her, Maidie had snatched up the broom and was pursuing the terrified bird round and round the room, beating at it.

"Stop, Maidie," said Laura firmly, taking the broom out of her hands almost by force. "You go and sit down. I'll get it out. And if anyone's going to die, it'll be me, because I opened the window."

White-faced and panting, Maidie at last was quiet, and, exiling Mother Brindle to the shed from the sink-board on which she was crouched with lashing tail, Laura drew all the shades except the one at the open window and soon had the junco out in the sunshine again. Then, seeing that Maidie's fear was real, she made her a cup of tea, and as she drank it her color came back, but she was not reassured.

"Mark my words, death will enter this house, Laura, before the year is out. I never knew it to fail. I'm the oldest, so it may well be me, and remember, if I die I'll always blame you for it. If it's you, you'll have brought it on yourself by your headstrong ways. Perhaps it's only a warning. Thank you anyhow for the tea."

After years of living together, Laura knew her sister-in-law so well that she could almost read her thoughts: If Laura died, Gus could probably be persuaded to sell the farm and they would go back to the village. But who would do the cooking, the washing, the ironing, the sweeping, the darning, the patching, and all the rest? On the whole, Maidie preferred to have her stay alive.

A shadow seemed to have fallen across the brightness of the morning, and to escape from it Laura turned to the chores she liked best: the trip with garbage to the pail at the corner of the barn, and the burning of the trash. Every morning she was free then to be outdoors for a few minutes without neglecting her work. The garbage was quickly disposed of, and next came the satisfaction of burning the papers. When she had put them in the old battered incinerator, and after several false starts had succeeded in setting them alight, she stood back. No one was supposed to leave even a caged fire like this, especially on a hilltop where the flames were often flattened out by the wind, and even torn from their roots and sent in burning tongues out over the snow.

Laura stood guard, her eyes resting on the beloved landscape. High Hill lay like a recumbent lion, in winter a lion of marble, with head reared high. Their farm had been the first cleared land, the first stand of buildings to be erected. Laura's great-grandfather, Alexander King, coming up from Massachusetts at the beginning of the nineteenth century to settle in virgin country, had seen it from the shores of what was now called High Hill Pond.

"That's the place for me," he was said to have exclaimed, "where the sun comes early and the frost comes late." It was also said that he had remarked, "When I build a house no one shall overlook me." Certainly there was in him a sort of pride, for while others were content to build their houses of wood, he must use the rock of the hilltop itself, splitting it into blocks of hewn granite for his house and then building a barn so large that people had prophesied that it would always be half empty. Yet he had filled it.

If Alexander King boasted, it was in granite and

oak beams, in thick stone walls and wide fields, not in words. High Farm, crowning the lion-headed hill, was his boast, proclaiming the imagination, the boldness, and perhaps the self-sufficiency of its builder. Even today, in its decline, one felt the nobility of its conception, stark and unyielding, the strong center of the wide horizon. It was for this, the work of his hands and will and passionate desire, that people had half-mockingly, half-enviously called the first owner King Pin, and the succeeding masters of High Farm had always had a recognized position in the community.

Yet King Pin nearly ended his life a childless man. He had three sons and a daughter, and two of the boys and the girl died of diphtheria in one terrible week. The remaining boy was dying, too. The doctor from the coast town said that there was nothing further he could do to save him. But then—how often Laura had heard the story—there was a knock on the door, and when her great-grandmother opened it an Indian stood outside with a load of ax handles and splint baskets on his back. He was wearing white men's clothes, but he had a silver buckle in his old hat and a blanket of worn rabbit skins on his back. Even before they told him, he seemed to know the trouble they were in.

"You let me," he said, looking King Pin in the eye. And King Pin, who in all his days had never relegated a decision to anyone, gave what was left of his last son's life into Indian Joe's hands.

Laura did not know exactly how the cure had been effected. There had been hours in a sweat-house built hastily under Indian Joe's directions. And at some time a split-open chicken had been applied to the boy's throat. Certainly Indian Joe had chanted and prayed heathenish prayers, and at last had carried the child back to his bed, covered him over with his own rabbit-skin robe, sat down on the floor by his side, and told the parents not to return until morning.

And when they came back at dawn the boy was weak, but the disease was gone.

King Pin offered the Indian money or horses or cattle in reward, but all he would take was enough land in a corner of the Big Field on which to build a cabin for his family. He had lived and died there, and had been King Pin's right-hand man in everything, the only human being he ever consulted. But when Indian Joe died, his family moved away. Laura's father, a young man at the time, never knew just why.

"I did my best to make him stay. If it hadn't been for old Indian Joe, I wouldn't be here, nor you either, Laura, and there'd be strangers at High Farm. But his son had taken some kind of notion. I couldn't budge him. And I've always regretted it. After they left, things never went quite so well." And Laura's father would take her in to the parlor to see the silver buckle from Indian Joe's hat, which the old man had given him before he died. It was always kept polished and had the place of honor on the table, where it still lay, to be admired but not to be touched by the children.

As the years passed, since the soil was good, other people settled along the ridge, and at the shoulders of the hill a crossroad was built plunging steeply down into the valley on either side. Today the West Road had two prosperous farms on it, but the East Road, which had originally been more thickly settled, was almost deserted.

Beyond the crossroads, the High Farm lane began between stone walls set widely apart, and rose, often over slides of granite, to the buildings which crowned the lion's head, staring across at Mt. Washington. Only the sun and wind, the rain and snow came freely here—above all, the wind.

This morning Laura saw that the snow was everywhere rippled in sand patterns like the shores of a sea whose waters were space. On the roofs, much of it had melted, leaving black winglike diagonals of wet shingles. She glanced again at the incinerator. Only ghostly bits of paper were stirring at the bottom. Her excuse for staying out any longer was gone, and as she turned away, the shed door opened and the three children appeared with their sleds.

"Have a good time!" she called and they raised red mittens in acknowledgment. She forgot the passing shadow which the omen of the bird had cast across the morning. A new year was beginning!

That very afternoon, while the children were down the road skating with friends on one of the new farm ponds, something occurred, small perhaps in itself, but giving Laura great pleasure, not unmixed with pain. Jim Clark, the veterinarian, drove up in his jeep for another look at the sheep, which he had already dosed once and which seemed to be on the mend. Only one ewe, the sickest, had taken the other path and died.

Gus was glad to see Jim and asked him in. He had a stranger with him, a stocky, moon-faced man, probably in his fifties, but it was hard to tell his age for his face was unwrinkled and there was no gray in the black straightness of his hair. Jim introduced him, but Laura, busy with coffee for the guests, only caught the name "Little Joe." She wondered who he could be. He didn't look like anyone she knew, and she was quite sure that she had never seen him before. Yet something in her memory seemed to stir.

A small cough from Maidie warned her that she was showing too much interest in the stranger. Maidie was still coy in her own conversation with men, and more than once Laura had been embarrassed by her elderly flirtatiousness, just as Maidie disapproved of Laura's straightforward friendliness.

Briefly, while the coffee was boiling, the three men went out to the barn, and when they came in again they were still talking about the sheep, which apparently were coming along.

"I say they need more outdoor air, Mr. Clark,"

broke in Maidie in her most ladylike voice. "Don't you agree with me?"

"Better wait till March, and then if we have a thaw Gus might let them out for a little. What you need around here, Gus, is more help. And I've brought you the right man."

Gus stiffened.

"I can handle things myself," he said, but before he could go on Jim interrupted, laughing, but a little embarrassed, as though he'd promised to put in a good word for a friend, and was doing his best.

"Sure you can, Gus," he said heartily. "Sure you can. You do fine. But Little Joe here'd make things a lot easier. Since the sawmill closed down, he's helped me more than once, so I know he's a good man with animals. And didn't you tell me, Little Joe, you'd worked on a farm?"

"Ayeh. All my life, round Orono and Old Town," the other man said slowly. "But my wife's dead and my kids are married. I'd work for you cheap, Mr. Treadwell, for just enough to keep going. This is where I was born."

Laura swung around, her brown eyes glowing. Of course! Little Joe! He'd be Indian Joe's grandson!

"Indian Joe," she exclaimed in a low voice.

But the man heard and nodded.

"Sure. He was my grandpa. Pa cleared out when Grandpa died. I was six years old, but I remember. I've always wanted to come back."

"Your folks lived down in the cabin at the corner

of the Big Field," Gus said. "Not much left of it now. All fallen into the cellar."

"I know," said the man, "but I could build it again. Chimney's standing."

"Maybe you could, but you aren't going to," said Gus. Then his words sounded too harsh even in his own ears. "I can't afford hired help and that's an end to it," he added.

"That's all right," said Little Joe with a smile.

The coffee was ready and Laura passed round the cups with a plate of doughnuts. When she came to Little Joe, she held out her hand.

"When I was a little girl, I heard so much about your grandfather," she said. "Would you like to see his silver buckle? It's in the parlor."

"That will do, Laura," said Maidie sharply, as though speaking to a child who was talking too much, but today for the first time in all these years under the same roof, Laura was out of hand, and never glanced in her direction. Gus opened his mouth as though to speak and then thought better of it.

Little Joe seemed to notice nothing.

"Sure," he said, heaving himself out of his chair, and, putting down his coffee cup on the kitchen table, he followed Laura into the cold parlor.

For a little while they stood in silence, looking at the buckle in his thick hand.

"He could do a lot besides cure people," Little Joe said at last. "Did you ever hear—" and he began to tell her stories of strange occurrences, most of them

43

new to Laura. She listened breathlessly, but all too soon Jim Clark called from the kitchen, "Guess we ought to get going, Little Joe."

The Indian put the buckle down carefully and stood silent for a moment longer looking out toward the hills. The sky had darkened, gray-black over the white snow. The storm which the moon had promised would come soon.

Suddenly he turned and smiled at Laura.

"Don't worry. We get this all fixed up like it used to be, when I come back."

Soon afterwards the men left, and Maidie started in on Laura's boldness, but Gus interrupted her.

"Oh, forget it! Little Joe's like one of her own folks, kind of. I wish I could hire him, Laura, but you know how we're fixed."

Laura touched his shoulder with her hand as she passed by, collecting cups.

"I know, Gus."

Probably Maidie saw, for now she repeated, "Yes, one of her own folks. I've heard it said those Indians who used to live up here were related to the family."

"I didn't mean that," Gus interrupted again, but Maidie went on with a little laugh, "Well, *I* mean it. They say the man who built here, the one they call King Pin, married a half-Indian woman. No wonder they chose Laura to play Pocahontas in the school graduation play! There was quite a little talk about it at the time."

Laura could feel Maidie's eyes searching her face,

but with an effort she kept it expressionless. Her sister-in-law would have been surprised to know that it was pleasure which she was concealing. What Maidie had just said might be true or it might not be true. Her father had never spoken of it, but his silence might have sprung from a variety of causes. She hoped that Maidie was right. Indian blood would bind her even more closely to this land she so loved.

4

$\mathcal{T}$HAT YEAR, the snowstorms were incessant. They began soon after the middle of November and seemed
only to pause to take breath before beginning once
more. The road crews were in the snowplows and sand
trucks at all hours of the day and night, until the
men looked like soldiers in the front lines during a
bombardment, unshaven and red-eyed from lack of
sleep.

Matt Armstrong, who had the concession for the
High Hill district, rigged up a contrivance to wake
him up when necessary.

"I just nailed a tin pie-plate to a board outside my
bedroom window," he told people. "When it gets
filled with snow it tips the board and that rings a
bell by my bed, and I don't have to keep awake half
the night to see what the weather's doing, by golly."

At one or two in the morning, Laura would hear

49

the slow approach of the plow, with its galaxy of lights, struggling up their lane between the stone walls. Legally, Matt might have saved himself that last wind-drifted stretch, for the public road stopped at their gate, but among neighbors such a thing was unthinkable. The road crews were not alone in finding it a rugged winter. The school-bus driver had a good deal to say on the subject. There were days when he couldn't get through and the children missed school, and once the bus was stuck in a drift, and the Treadwell three had to walk to the nearest house with a telephone. Gus went to their rescue on snowshoes and brought them safely home, leading the way with Alvinia riding pick-a-back, Paul next on the extra pair of snowshoes, and Mildred in the rear, following without too much trouble along the packed trail.

"I don't know why I didn't have the snowshoes," she complained as soon as she entered the kitchen.

"You're lighter than Paul," her father told her.

"Yes, but she's older," Maidie chimed in as though to settle the matter.

For her, doing so little, the winter dragged interminably, and she railed at the monotony. But to Laura no two storms were alike. Some fell in feather-light flakes; some came driven by a screaming wind; some were combined with ice or hoarfrost. And there were great displays in the sky of sundogs by day and northern lights by night, and once there was a thunderstorm, loud and blinding through the falling snow. When she was young, she had never felt isolated at High Farm. She had been content to stay fixed, aware as she was of the journeys of sun and moon and stars, of the winds and clouds, and the shadows of clouds, and the shadows of hills and of buildings, and the movements of seasons and birds. She felt these things unconsciously and with them the passing of time, too, which had left behind it at High Farm so many accumulated layers of hard work and happiness. But this heritage now was being overlaid by something else, a sense of failure and bitterness.

"You have everything and I have nothing," Maidie had once said to Laura, and Laura had thought, "What have I? You have taken everything." A threat hung over the place and everyone in it, and this winter the sense of coming disaster had darkened as a cloud darkens just before the beginning of a thunderstorm. She had never heard the apple trees groan as much as they did now to herald a coming storm, particularly at night. At night, too, from the beechwood below the south cliff came the hooting of the owls, and sometimes there were cries that were not the wind.

Slowly the winter, storm by storm, wore down the nerves of half the garrison at High Farm, beginning with Maidie and her shadow, Mildred, and ending with Gus, who became increasingly irritable, even once in a while with Maidie. Paul and Alvinia were little changed, and Laura looked from the cold windows each morning with fresh eagerness to see what the day might bring forth. If Maidie's strength lay in the secrets she hoarded, bringing them out in the ripeness of time, Laura's was in sky and sea and hills, in the wonders of light and the mysteries of darkness.

She needed what strength she could find, for in the crowded kitchen she lived a lonely life. To give of herself was essential to her nature, but a spring with no outlet must in the end become a swamp, and she felt a slow disintegration taking place in spite of all her hopeful resolutions. As for Maidie, boredom made her prickly. When the children were home she had a willing pupil in Mildred, learning how to avoid anything she didn't wish to do.

"Please help me clear the table," Laura said one morning after breakfast. At once Mildred glanced at her aunt.

"Laura, let the poor child alone! You know it gives her indigestion to be hurried," Maidie instantly defended.

Or perhaps in the evening Laura suggested some game which they might all play. Maidie would have none of it.

"Mildred and I are going to play checkers, and the winner gets chocolate peppermints."

Alvinia was part of this inner circle, but on its outskirts. Even at six, by temperament she was a worker, not a shirker. It was her father whom she followed about everywhere, lending a hand surprisingly efficient for one so small, but sometimes she would help Laura, too. As for Paul, his indifference appeared to extend to them all. More than once after his teacher had written that, in spite of some improvement, he was still failing in arithmetic, Laura tried to help him. She would sit beside him at the kitchen table, and very slowly and clearly explain the problem. He might seem to listen.

"I see!" he would exclaim. "Thanks."

But he had not listened. He had only been waiting for her to go away. And when he did the problem over, he made the same mistakes that he had made before.

Sometimes Laura felt like a ghost. When she said something, it often happened that no one answered. As the winter went on, more and more she became silent. Her large, dark eyes, which Maidie had once likened to a cow's, deriding what she secretly admired, had an almost frightened look. The sense of promise which she had felt at New Year's was growing dim.

Meanwhile, as January went on, and the days grew longer and the cold grew stronger and the thaws came and went and the icicles hung sharper and brighter than glass fangs from the eaves, the spirit of the household deteriorated even further. A teasing mood seized Aunt Maidie and her attendant Mildred. Mean little tricks were played, and there was often an ugly sound of giggling in the kitchen. Most frequently Paul or Laura was the butt, yet sometimes Alvinia and Gus had their turn. Maidie was careful not to go very far with Gus, but she had not forgiven his interference after Little Joe's visit, and now and then she allowed herself to give him a little jab. If turned on, the teasers were all innocence. "Why, I didn't mean anything!" or "Can't you take a joke?" and then, catching one another's eye, they would change their laughter to coughing.

One Sunday afternoon this form of boredom reached its climax. It was snowing outside, the sort of wet windy snow which held no invitation for going out. Paul, as usual when he was home, had come down into the kitchen, followed by the Wabasso, who, after sitting staring at each of the family in turn, had taken his place with the other animals under the stove, they as usual making wide room for him. The three children were busy at scrapbooks, each with a saucer of flour paste and a small pile of old Christmas cards and pictures cut out from discarded copies of the Sears catalogues.

For a little while things went well. Then Mildred began to suggest trading some of her near-duplicates, and soon there were loud protests from Alvinia, who had been overreached. After these had been quieted, there was more or less busy silence again.

The next interruption was the sound of a slap, followed by a screech from Mildred.

"You stop that, Paul!"

"Then you stop stealing my best pictures!"

"Did not!"

"Did, too!"

"I never did, Aunt Maidie!"

"Of course you didn't, darling. Paul made a mistake. Say you're sorry, Paul. It isn't nice for a boy to slap a girl anyhow."

"But she did take my pictures."

"Say you're sorry."

"I won't."

"You must, Paul. Aunt Maidie wants you to."

Gus was napping on the cot beyond the stove and never woke up, but Laura, who had taken no part in the conversation up to now, made a decision.

"It's almost four," she said, trying to speak with an authority she didn't feel. "Why don't we all have a cup of chocolate? Will you get the milk from the shed, Paul? And Mildred, you can bring out the best cups."

It was always Maidie who suggested chocolate, making a party of it. She glared at Laura for daring to take over her prerogative. Paul got up unwillingly, making a great show of gathering up his pictures first and putting them beyond Mildred's reach, and Mildred, her face in its halo of light hair looking pinched, said under her breath, "I'll get even with you!" while Alvinia steadily went on with her pasting.

It was not a very successful party, but it did serve to make the afternoon pass and there was no more open bickering. After Laura had washed the cups, she brought out the ironing board and got to work on her endless task. This afternoon she stood as she did so often, her back to the kitchen, ironing with her old-fashioned electric iron, and now and then glancing out of the window. She was tired, as always at this time of day, and her mind was almost a blank, when suddenly she was brought back to the present by hearing Maidie behind her exclaim with unusual sharpness, "Mildred!"

At the same moment Laura felt cold air about her ankles and, turning, saw Mildred standing in the open kitchen door, which was never used at this time of the year.

"Shut the door!" Laura called. But the child seemed not to have heard. She stood staring off toward the horizon, her young figure outlined against the falling snow.

At that moment the Wabasso came out from under the stove and began to move toward the door, his nose held high, sniffing the air. At the same time, Paul looked up from his scrapbook and with a cry jumped to his feet, upsetting his chair. Before he could reach the Wabasso, the rabbit sprang for the open doorway, shot past Mildred, who had never moved, and disappeared.

A moment later Laura found herself also outdoors. A little distance away Paul was standing, half hidden by the drifting flakes so that he seemed almost a shadow, around which a spirit was dancing. For the Wabasso was circling him, sometimes leaping high into the air, sometimes pausing to stand upright, sometimes frisking and skipping, all with an indefinable air of gaiety. But when the boy reached down to touch him, he suddenly disappeared into the curtained snow.

"Come back, come back!" Paul called. "Come back!"

But though Paul and Laura both called and went here and there—to the lilac bush, to the chicken house, to the tool shed—the Wabasso had disappeared, and at last Laura insisted that they must go in. Paul seemed not to see or hear her, so she put her cold hands on his shoulders and he came with her unresisting.

Mildred still stood in the doorway, watching. She stepped back to make room for them, but Paul did not seem to know that she was there. It was Laura who said indignantly, "Mildred! You did that on purpose!"

"I did not!" retorted Mildred. "How did I know the old thing would come out from under the stove?"

"Of course the child didn't know," came Maidie's voice from the rocking chair. "But close the door, dearie, the cold air's blowing on Auntie."

And when the door had been closed, and Laura, shivering violently, had pushed the kettle forward, Maidie turned to Paul, who was standing by the west window, his face blindly pressed to the pane.

"I'm real sorry, Paul," she said, "but accidents will happen and I'm sure Mildred's sorry, too. A rabbit's only a rabbit when all's said and done."

Paul made no answer and after a moment she added, "I never liked the queer way that rabbit stared at me. Laura, I'll have a cup of tea, since you're making it."

Laura nodded, but the first cup, with plenty of milk and sugar in it, she made Paul drink.

"Maybe we can get you another rabbit somewhere," she said in a low voice.

This time he glared at her.

"I know it wouldn't be the same," she added helplessly. The old frustration rose up, like a sickness through her body, as she took a cup of tea to Maidie. All her children were strangers. She could do nothing for them. Slowly she went back to the ironing board.

In the press of her feelings, she had not missed Alvinia, but now the little girl came in from the shed, wearing one of her father's old mackinaws almost trailing on the ground and all but hiding her hands, in one of which she was carrying a small basket of eggs. Her coming was usually a forerunner of her father's, and sure enough, Gus followed, smelling of the barn and of new milk.

He noticed nothing out of the way, but Alvinia's blue eyes were sharper.

"Mamma's crying!" she exclaimed. "Mamma's crying right on the pillow slips!"

"You women been quarrelling?" Gus demanded.

Laura went on with her work. It was Maidie who answered, "Mercy no, Gus! It was just a little accident. Mildred opened the door to look out a moment and Paul's rabbit hopped off. It was one of those things."

"Too bad," said Gus. "Likely he'll come back when he's hungry. Buck up, Paul, and stop looking as if you'd lost your last friend."

Paul said dully, "He was my only friend."

Gus clapped his son on the back, half in sympathy, half in irritation. "Snap out of it. You've got to learn to take the bitter with the sweet."

He sat down, pulling out his pipe, and his eye came to rest on Mildred, combing out her fair hair at the little mirror between the two windows.

"As for you, young lady," he said, "you be more careful what you're doing in the future."

Mildred turned round and smiled at her father. In a voice of honey, she said, "Oh, I *will* be, Dad! I'm *so* sorry."

"There's Auntie's dear girl," approved Maidie from her corner.

Beyond the lighted windows the snow was turning blue in the early dusk, and somewhere the Wabasso was tasting the joys of his new freedom.

5

$\mathcal{T}$HEY WERE GONE. The whole family except Laura had departed for town in the old car, with Gus and Maidie in the front seat, and the three children in the back. They needed to buy sugar and coffee and tea, flour and molasses, for winter supplies were getting low.

"I don't like to have you here all alone, Laura," said Gus as they were leaving. Before Laura could answer, Maidie spoke up for her.

"Someone has to stay to look after things," she said, "and besides, there isn't room."

"One of the children could stay."

There was an outcry from Mildred in the back seat.

Laura protested. "I don't mind staying a bit, Gus. Thank you for thinking of it. And do give your mother my love," and she stepped back from the car and stood smiling and waving as Gus drove away.

At that moment she had no plans, but how quickly they came to her! She went back into the kitchen, with its stale air and smell of cooking. Rapidly she slipped a couple of faggots into the firebox and half closed the dampers so that they would burn slowly. Then she went through the shed into the barn.

She loved the barn, with its high rafters and its double line of braced beams. There was no other barn in the county whose upper structure had that flying look. The light was soft and golden. In their big pen the sheep stood and lay drowsily about. Two or three of them already had dropped their lambs, but no more were expected just now. As she spoke to them, several bleated in answer and moved up to the bars to be patted. She had always had a way with animals, and now she stood for a few minutes talking to the flock, praising the lambs, encouraging the expectant ewes. She saw that in the excitement of going to town Paul had forgotten to renew their drinking water, so she pumped a few pails for them at the kitchen sink, taking pleasure in the strong kerplunk, kerplunk of the handle and the spilling out of the cold, clear stream as she never did when doing her household chores. Rex followed her about, standing at her side, wagging his tail a little as he looked benignly at the sheep. He had been a good sheep dog in his day, but was too old for the work now. Gus often said he must get another dog, but so far he had not done so, perhaps because he did not like to do away with Rex.

From her stall, the cow mooed for attention, and from one of the other stalls, most of them empty now, her calf bawled, protesting the separation. Laura went to both, patting their hollow foreheads. The calf tried to suck her fingers. "You'll be fed when they get back," she promised, and her words reminded her that she did not have much time in which she might do as she pleased.

"I'll see if I can find any trace of the Wabasso," she thought. "Poor Paul has hunted and hunted, but perhaps on this fine day I might see him."

She put on her coat, tied an old scarf about her head, and took down a pair of snowshoes from the pegs on the shed wall where they had hung ever since she could remember. Outside she buckled them on slowly and carefully, for the straps were stiff with age. Then she straightened up and looked about her. North, south, east, or west, into which beauty should she go?

The sun was just low enough to set the particles of ice on the surface sparkling in little jets of red, violet, green, and gold fire which had the colors but none of the softness of the rainbow.

Old Rex leaned against her, but she led him back to the shed door and put him indoors, much against his will. Walking had become difficult for him and she wanted to go fast. It was so warm that she did not put on her mittens.

"I'll go to Indian Joe's place," she thought, partly because she would have the sun at her back and partly because her memories had been stirred by Little Joe's visit.

She started off with a long swinging stride. It was some time since she had been on snowshoes, but, like swimming, the art is not one which the body forgets. As she walked, she looked about her with delight. The sky was everywhere clear, and over the white lip of field the eye travelled for miles and miles across the coastal country, snow-patterned with the dark green of forests and the bright blue of the far-off sea. A feather of smoke to the northeast marked where a little city lay, unseen, but not forgotten in her thoughts. A train, smaller than a ladybug, passed between hummocks of woodland, Boston-bound, and once a plane, almost invisible itself, left a thin white arch of vapor across the sky.

Close at hand she saw Mother Brindle stretched out, sinuous and watchful on top of the nearest stone wall.

Smiling, Laura went on, preceded by her shadow. It was a good day for snowshoeing, and she went easily, looking about. Here a far-blown beech leaf, bent over like a little toad, scrabbled across her path. Sometimes where the snow was thinner, she stopped to see the tunnels of the field mice, standing up like veins of life in the chilly whiteness. Two juncos flew by overhead.

Now the slope of the hill became steeper. Below and along one side of the square Big Field, to which the snow had lent once more its old clean-cut lines, there was waste land belonging to their former neighbors, now growing up to pines and alders. When she was a girl this was pasture land, and from it all summer long had risen the sound of the cowbells. At the bottom of the Big Field, against this second growth, rose the chimney of what had been Indian Joe's cabin. The roof had fallen in, and the log walls, long ago rotted, were tumbled in a disintegrating heap. Everywhere there were rabbit tracks, in and out of the ruins. She called and called, but the Wabasso did not come, and after a while she gave up. Now that the adjoining fields were overgrown, there was no longer any view from the site. It was a melancholy spot heavy with the sense of the passing of time, and time in its meaner aspect, not so much as the destroyer as the belittler. Laura's mood of excitement turned sober as she stood looking round her, and, unbidden, she remembered the bird flying about the kitchen and how she had taken upon herself the omen of death.

"I'm getting just as shabby as everything else at High Farm," she thought. "I'm resentful and sorry for myself. I'm surprised that Gus puts up with me at all."

But she had not come here to think about her troubles. She was paying a visit to the spirit of Indian Joe. In this little cabin great wonders had taken place. Her father had forgotten many of the stories he may have heard as a boy, but Little Joe remembered them, and had told them to her as they stood together in the parlor at the farm.

His grandfather, he said, could read the future on

the shoulder bones of animals. He could draw sickness out of a body in the form of a mouse, and call up terrible winds which shook the cabin. Sometimes spirit animals talked to him from the darkness of the roof, and once he struck his knife into the air and showed it to the little boy covered with blood.

"He was a great medicine man," Little Joe said.

And yet he could not heal his wife, Abbie Neptune, when her time came, nor change his son's longing for the sea. Perhaps these tales of Little Joe's were mostly made up out of the imaginings of a six-year-old child. Yet part of Laura believed that they were true. The last scene of all she remembered most clearly.

"I went in to see him," Little Joe had told her. "Grandpa was lying there on his bed, with his eyes closed. Over him was the old rabbit-skin robe he always used. For a while he didn't say nothing. Then without opening his eyes he said, 'You're the one will come back, Little Joe. You and me.' That's all he said. Then Ma pushed me out of the room and a little later they told me he was dead. Pretty soon my family packed up and went away. But I always wanted to come back."

Laura gave a little shiver. She had been standing for a long time without moving, and as the sun sank the ruins became lapped by the shadow of the hilltop, which stretched above them, a blue dome against the softening western sky.

Putting on her mittens, she started home along the trail which her snowshoes had made. The slope was steeper than she had remembered, or perhaps she was growing older. From here she could not see the house, hidden by the curve of the land, but she thought that she caught a glimpse of smoke dissipating in the clear air to show that the fire in the kitchen had not gone out.

Suddenly, from above her she heard the sound of Rex barking.

"That's funny," she thought, but at first she did not pay much attention to it.

In this colder air of late afternoon, the snow underfoot began to squeak with each step. She was listening to it with pleasure when a large rabbit went past her, coming apparently from the ruins of the cabin, where it must have crouched hidden during her visit there. But why, having lain safe for so long, did it now come out into the open and make, not for the near-by woods beyond the wall, but for the shelterless field and the dangerous proximity of a human being?

Unless, of course, it was the Wabasso after all, and she began to call his name, until, without a glance, the creature disappeared over the curve of the hill.

"One rabbit looks much like another," she thought. "If it *is* the Wabasso, I hope he knows how to take care of himself. He doesn't act like it."

The sky was fading to white, lighter now than the shadowed snow. It would soon turn dark. From the farm above her she still heard Rex's barking, muffled by the shed in which he was shut, but somehow frantic. It made her uneasy. She had never before

heard Rex bark when left alone. He was a quiet, man-
nerly old dog, not given to hysterics. She didn't like it.

Laura quickened her pace, breathing hard. Now
she could see the tops of the elms and the roofs and
chimneys of High Farm. Just then, moved by some
impulse, she glanced at the trail she was travelling.
Two tracks had crossed it. One was that of the rabbit
which had gone by her, only a few minutes earlier.
The animal was no longer running easily, as when she
had seen it, but was going at the top of its speed, in
great leaps, dodging, too, as it ran. Beginning at
Laura's old trail, which it had evidently been following, another track had turned aside in pursuit of the
rabbit, and it was this track which made her catch her
breath. The pad marks were so large and so far apart
that she could not imagine what animal had made
them. The lesser question as to why even the Wabasso
had come so close to an enemy in the open gave way
to this other. What had been following along her
trail?

For the first time in all her life on High Hill, Laura
felt the chill of actual physical fear. She did not wait
to study the drama in the snow. With primitive
immediacy she knew that she must get back to the
shelter of the farm as quickly as she could. Now she
was really running, but without giving way to the
panic which seemed one step behind her. Whatever
it was that had followed her had come out of the
overgrown meadow land, crossed the stone wall, and
joined her trail high up on the hill at a point not far

below the farmhouse. She knew that footprints in the snow may seem larger than they really are, but these were enormous. Wild dog? Wolf? There were always stories. Mountain lion? People in lonely places claimed to have heard and seen them, but couldn't prove their claims. Had it been hunting her or only been curious? Mountain lions are said not to attack men, but others say that they will when hungry. After nearly three months of snow, this one would be hungry.

Here Laura cut across the field toward the farm; the shortest way was best, and those tracks pacing by hers daunted her. What would have happened if the rabbit hadn't blundered across the creature's path and shifted its object of pursuit? The sun had just sunk, and the whole world was one chalk-white shadowless stare.

Fumbling at the stiffened straps, turning her head to look back over her shoulder, Laura knelt at the shed door, worried off her snowshoes, and blindly pushed up the latch. As she closed the door behind her, Rex leaped upon her, almost knocking her over in his relief. He at least had no doubt that she had been in great danger.

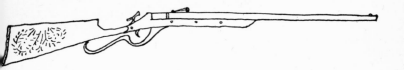

6

*W*HEN A LITTLE AFTER DARK the car drove into the dooryard, Laura had not finished the preparations for supper. She was very seldom late, and Maidie, hungry and disappointed, remarked, as she put down on the sink-board the small package she was carrying, "Supper not ready yet?"

"It will be by the time you've taken off your things and washed up," said Laura cheerfully. "Did you have a nice visit with your mother?"

Maidie's answer was lost in the arrival of the rest of the family, all lugging in staples. The trip had done them good, and even Paul looked as though he had enjoyed himself. The children were fond of their grandmother, and a visit to her was always a treat. She had reached the age when she ate only what she enjoyed, and as that was mostly starches and sweets, her pantry was a treasure house of cakes and cookies and rows of preserves and jellies, with which she was most liberal.

Now Maidie produced a jar and put it down beside the busy Laura.

"Ma sent you some of her spiced peaches," she said affably.

"Oh, that *was* kind of her!"

Few presents came Laura's way, and her heart was warm with gratitude to Mrs. Treadwell.

Supper was a cheerful meal. Everyone was a little excited, and even Paul had a tale to tell of a boy he knew who had won the hundred-yard race at the inter-school meet in Rockland.

"And Red's one of the smallest boys in class," he said, "but can he make those legs of his go!"

Listening to Paul's talk of races, Laura thought of the rabbit track which had crossed the trail of the unknown marauder. There across the snowy field had been a race of a different kind. And Laura was afraid that the little runner had lost it, and that the Wabasso —for only an animal whose instincts had been blurred by captivity could behave as that rabbit had behaved— must now be dead.

She listened to them all, smiling and nodding, saying very little. Even when Maidie remarked to Mildred, "Dearie, why don't you fetch Grandma's spiced peaches? I left them by the sink. They'll taste good with beans and cole slaw," she still smiled and nodded, though for a moment she felt that something was being jerked out of her hands. Surely, she rebuked herself, she would not have eaten the treat by herself! She would have served it, just like this, some night, but she would have enjoyed being the one to choose the night.

Perhaps Maidie herself felt a little guilty, for after supper she did something which she knew gave Laura pleasure and which she could rarely be prevailed upon to do. Sitting back from the littered supper table, she began to sing, first "Rock of Ages" and "The Old Rugged Cross" and then "I Was Seeing Nelly Home." Gus, who had been lighting his pipe, put it down and at once took up the tune, singing bass, and halfway through the first hymn Paul's tenor joined in. They all had good voices, but Maidie's was really beautiful, clear and cool, like a young girl's. The nonsingers of the family listened, their faces turning soft and happy.

Suddenly the moment was torn across as old Rex came out from under the stove, with a howl. Every hair on his body was standing on end, and his dim eyes were glaring.

"For gosh sakes, what's the matter?" Gus was startled.

"Something's after the sheep," said Laura. "I saw tracks this afternoon. Big ones."

"What were you doing?" Maidie began, always suspicious, always prying.

But Gus heaved to his feet.

"I'll take the gun and see."

By this time Laura was taking down her sweater from the door.

"No need for you to come," he said as he went out.

But Laura paid no attention.

"He said you weren't to go," Maidie shrilled.

"I'd better," said Laura. "Keep the children in, Maidie. It's big."

Gus had closed the door on the howling Rex, but Laura took a firm hold on the old dog's collar with her left hand, and went out with him into the shed. It was empty. Gus had taken the shotgun from the high pegs where her father had always kept it beyond reach of small hands. The outside door was open and clapping in the night wind.

As Laura passed by the chopping block, she jerked free the light ax and, still holding firmly to Rex's collar, went out.

Since afternoon the clouds had come up, and now the wind was driving them across the waning moon, which stood halfway down the sky in the west. Alternating moonlight and shadow swept the fields, so that everything seemed to be moving.

First here, then there, Laura thought she saw a darker creeping but couldn't be sure. It was hard even to make out Gus, but Rex pulled her toward him. The dog had stopped howling now, though he still growled and whined. Laura whistled to Gus, not wanting to meet a load of buckshot, and knowing that he had had little experience with guns or wild animals. But he had plenty of courage. That was why she

78

had to be with him. If the thing which had left those tracks were wounded, it would attack, and if it attacked, Gus would need all the help she could bring and perhaps more.

But that night, no such crisis arose. They could never afterward say whether or not they had even seen anything, but several times Gus fired at what might have been a more palpable shadow, and Laura felt almost certain that something had moved down the lane behind a stone wall.

Anyway, the prowler departed. That much they could measure by the barometer of Rex, who became gradually quiet, rumbling a little in his throat as he sniffed about rather vaguely in the snow. But when Gus and Laura turned at last to go back, relaxed, and beginning to talk in low voices, they were startled by a definite motion in the shadow of the barn.

"Don't!" Laura said breathlessly, feeling Gus start to raise the shotgun. "It's one of the children." Then Alvinia ran up, stocky and stalwart.

"What are you doing here?" Gus demanded in the voice he used only for Alvinia.

"I came out to see if you were all right," she said. "Mamma was scared."

Gus gave a chuckle.

"Mamma wasn't scared," he told Alvinia. "She just wanted to see the excitement."

Alvinia said nothing but, taking his free hand, walked along between her father and mother, skipping sedately. Laura's heart felt a pang of pride. Where

Alvinia's love was concerned, she could not be deceived. But she could hold her tongue.

Their return to the kitchen was greeted by a hubbub of exclamations and questions.

"I didn't see any reason why Alvinia shouldn't go if you did," Maidie told Laura, and Laura said nothing. Maidie would never hear the truth in a human voice, never recognize danger as little Alvinia could hear it and know it, and now it no longer mattered. If the animal had been what Laura thought, it might well be twenty miles away by morning when the sun rose out of the sea. People said such creatures ranged far and wide, and often never returned to the place where they had been seen. The shooting had scared this one off, probably forever.

But if Laura thought the situation was closed, she counted without Maidie. The excursion into the night, even the roar of the shotgun, had made very little impression on her. What she wanted to know was where Laura had been that afternoon, and why.

No sooner had Laura taken off her sweater and returned to the dishpan than Maidie was at her with the persistence of a fly in muggy weather.

"Where'd you go this afternoon?" she asked, coming up close to Laura, while she stared into the younger woman's face.

Laura went on with her work.

"For a walk," she answered. Confronted by those pouncing eyes, she could not force herself to be more explicit.

But the inquisition went on.

"Where'd you go for your walk?"

"Oh, around."

"Round where?"

"Just getting some exercise."

"See anyone?"

Now Maidie's eyes were sharper than ever. She had a fixed idea that somehow in those lonely wind-swept fields Laura met someone, a man. How he would get there, she did not try to explain. Certainly Laura wrote almost no letters, scarcely ever used the telephone, and every letter she did write had its envelope carefully studied by Maidie; and every time she telephoned, Maidie was within hearing.

But Maidie had seen that on those rare occasions when Laura went out to walk, she came back looking refreshed and younger. To her mind, this could mean only one thing. Somehow, somewhere, Laura was meeting a man, and this thought was now clear in her eyes.

"No," said Laura. "Who would I see?"

"Oh, for gosh sake," exclaimed Gus from behind his pipe smoke, his head against the wall. "Can't you women stop your everlasting gab?"

"Why do you listen, then?" Maidie retorted.

After that, the family settled down. Gus dozed; on one side of the lamp Maidie put on her glasses and read the paper which she had brought back with her from town, while Laura, on the other side, busied herself with her endless darning. Farther down the kitchen table, Alvinia drew pictures of cows and sheep, Paul tried hopelessly to correct a smudged arithmetic paper, and Mildred turned the leaves of a new comic.

Outside, the wind howled about the stone farmhouse, but only Laura noticed it. Her dark eyes scarcely saw the needle busy at the rents in the stocking she held. Instead, she saw a sinewy figure, now in moonlight, now in shadow, slipping on soundless pads down the hill, through the thickets, stopping to eat snow when it was thirsty, lying in wait beside a moonlit rabbit runway, skirting a farm, and always working its way into the deeper woods, the wilder country from which the mountains rose, with the gales sweeping the snow from their summits in long streamers, white in the moonlight. Others might deny that the mountain lions were beginning to return to this country which had once been theirs, but in Laura's heart there was no doubt.

Lonely and beautiful, the creature moved through loneliness and beauty, and Laura watched it go.

The clock struck nine, and as usual it was Maidie who exclaimed, "Time to go to bed!" There was no protest from the children. Alvinia was already half asleep.

"I'll be up in a jiffy to hear your prayers," she added.

The girls slept in her room. "Might's well be where it's warm," she said. "I don't mind if they're more comfortable," and it was understood that Laura wasn't to put foot inside the door.

Paul long ago had refused to say his prayers out loud. "Kid stuff," he said. "I'm old enough to say them to myself," so if he said them at all, it was in the solitude of his bleak, bare room, where he lived alone now without the company of the Wabasso.

When the children were gone, Laura began the nightly ritual of putting Rex and Mother Brindle out for their run, hanging the damp dishcloths by the stove, trying the locks on the windows.

Maidie put down the newspaper with a rustle, and turned toward the cot where Gus sat, his head almost on his chest.

"Ma's not getting any younger, Gus," she began in her most reasonable voice. "I noticed today she's not steady on her feet. I think it's our duty to go down and look after her. I hear Ed Dean's shoe store could be bought, if anyone went about it the right way. He's getting awful rheumaticky. You could buy him out, maybe."

She waited, but Gus didn't say anything. He was listening, though. The two women could hear him sucking on his pipe.

Maidie went on, her voice rising a little.

"We'd have neighbors again, Gus. Something besides snowstorms and this awful wind blowing round the house day and night. The children wouldn't miss so much school, and you could go fishing again the way you used to when you was a boy. There wasn't anything you liked better than fishing! And all of us could go to church and socials like Christians, instead of perching up here like a passel of folks from a wrecked airplane on a mountaintop."

"Well, it's our living." Gus spoke for the first time, his voice noncommittal.

"Living?" Maidie repeated, and now the note of hysteria was plain. "What kind of living? I ask you that. What kind of living? Fields all run out to blueberries, and a handful of baaing, bleating, maggoty sheep! Call that a living? You could do a lot better in town. And as for the rest of us, we'd be living instead of dying, as we are up here. Dead alive, that's what we are, Gus!"

"Laura don't want to sell." Gus spoke in the same noncommittal voice, glancing at his wife, who was standing by the shed door, which she had just bolted for the night.

"Laura!" Maidie almost screamed the name. She was working herself into a passion, and the words tumbled out of her mouth. "Laura! We all have to do what Laura wants! Laura don't want to leave the farm, so we have to rot here with her! Laura wants to bring up her children like a lot of hillbillies, so here they are! Laura wants you to slave day and night so she can enjoy the view! Poor old Ma's got to die alone, so Laura can see the White Mountains when she's a mind to! Laura! Laura! It's always Laura!"

"After all, Laura owns the farm."

84

"And we're here on her charity. She never lets us forget that. Oh, she don't say it in words. She wouldn't dare. But she's proud like all the Kings. Will she do what we want? Not if you and I and the three children went down on our bended knees and begged her. Call them! I dare you to call them down! Well, what have you to say, Laura? Cat got your tongue? Why don't you answer?"

Laura stood staring and fixed by the door, one hand still on the latch. Her spirit was beaten upon by the torrent of Maidie's hatred. The woman was released from her daily pettiness. Now she drank deeply of the black springs. She who could not rhyme two words together was speaking the dark poetry of the blood. This was her core and center, and she took on beauty. Her face was a girl's face, lighted by a fire of feeling; her voice twanged like a harp string in jangled music.

But Laura was extinguished. Hate for her was poison, and her heart was sick in her drooping body.

Help came from an unexpected quarter. Perhaps Maidie's jibes during the winter had slowly unknotted the cord which bound Gus to his sister. Perhaps, though he had said nothing, he was grateful to Laura, who had run to his help, armed with an ax, when she thought that he was in danger. Perhaps he, too, loved the farm in his own way.

Now he said heartily, "You're right, of course, Maidie. Ma needs you, and it's your duty to go down and stay with her, for the winter, anyhow. I'm satisfied to be here, and so are the kids, Alvinia especially. You needn't worry about us."

7

Sometimes when things weren't quite to her satisfaction, Maidie had threatened to leave High Farm, but always Gus had begged her to stay, as though nothing could go on if she weren't there. Now for him casually to suggest her going, worse still, to say that he himself liked to be at the farm, was to Maidie a shock so violent that she was stunned. She thought she might have misunderstood him and said a little falteringly, "I'm glad you think we ought to go, Gus."

Gus answered in the same kindly voice, "Oh, Ma don't need both of us. It's your place to help her, now she's slowing up. An unmarried daughter ought to be home."

She gaped at him open-mouthed. Laura was sorry for her and turned her eyes away from her humiliation. She held no resentment: meanness such as Maidie's must be like hiccups, a sign of something wrong inside. But would this teach Maidie anything? Perhaps for a while, at least, she would be more careful.

Not for a moment did Laura allow herself to hope that Maidie could be got rid of so easily.

"I'm not strong enough to do housework!" Maidie began to cry in angry gulps, looking at Gus furiously. But he only reached for his tobacco pouch and filled his pipe.

"At least you can try," he said at last.

She jumped to her feet.

"You'll be sorry for this!" she shouted. "And you, too, Laura, you whited sepulcher! You put Gus up to this, but you'll rue the day!"

She waited a moment, but neither Gus nor Laura said anything or looked at her, and at last she slammed out of the room and they could hear her stamping up the stairs.

Still without speaking, the others finished closing the house for the night. An angry bawl from upstairs showed that Mildred had been alerted. Alvinia remained silent. She was fond of her aunt in a moderate way, but she was not a bawler, and so long as she was not separated from her father, her world remained secure.

As Gus and Laura passed by Maidie's room, a great switching about and banging proclaimed that she was packing for departure. Laura wondered what she would do with the stacks of old newspapers and magazines which she hoarded. She even saved the school papers as the children brought them home, neatly tied up with cord and arranged along one wall.

In their own room with the door closed, the sounds down the hall faded, and they got ready for bed as usual. Laura could not guess what Gus was feeling, and she dared not ask. She hoped that he would speak, but he said nothing, though before going to bed, moved by a sudden impulse, he put his hands on her shoulders and looked into her face as though he wished to say something or to ask her something, but in the end he only kissed her good night.

It must have been an hour later that they were awakened by a pounding on their door.

It was Maidie. She didn't wait to be told to come in, but burst into the room, as wild with fear as she had been with rage.

"The chimney's on fire!" she cried. "Gus, get up! The chimney's on fire!"

Her room felt hot as an oven as they ran in, barefooted. Everything was brightly lighted—Maidie never saved electricity—and the girls, sitting frightened in their cots, were flushed with the heat. Two half-filled suitcases lay open on Maidie's bed, and a steamer trunk stood beside it, nearly packed. On the floor, papers were scattered from the piles she had been burning. The stove was red-hot.

But what mattered was the loud roar in the chimney, which shook the air. It was a terrifying sound. The accumulation of years of soot was on fire. Gus acted quickly, ran down the stairs, and returned seconds later with a package of baking soda, which he threw into the stove, pushing up the red-hot latch with the heel of one of Maidie's shoes lying near by.

At once the fire, which had seemed so fierce, began to die down, but the flames in the chimney were not much affected. They roared on.

"We'd better go out and see how things are," Gus said. "Stop crying, Maidie. At this time of year, it probably won't set the house on fire. But get the children dressed to be on the safe side."

When Gus and Laura, their bare feet stuck in overshoes and with blankets wrapped about them, went outside, they found that the clouds, which had been gathering earlier in the evening, now covered the sky and a soft dry snow was falling. The only light came from the red pillar of fire standing up from the top of the chimney. Flakes of burning soot constantly rose from it like a flock of birds which settled on the roof and ground; but, meeting always with snow, they soon blackened and went out.

"Lucky it wasn't a dry spell," said Gus. "Paul, come on. We'll get the ladder out and have it handy. Laura, you can't help. Go in and make some coffee or we'll all catch our deaths of cold."

An hour later the fire had died away, the stove had returned to its accustomed dull blackness, and everyone was back in bed. Only the wind stirred about the warm bricks of the chimney, only an owl hooted from the woods.

For a little while, Laura lay awake with a thankful heart. She thought of how well Gus had handled the crisis. The house was saved, but what forces had taken hold of them all, she could not measure. A wind had picked them up, but from what quarter did it blow? Where would it set them down? Ever since the junco had flown into the kitchen on New Year's Day, one danger after another seemed shaking them loose from their old ways. It might be a good wind. Gus was more as he used to be in the early days of their marriage, but there was danger abroad. That she felt. Well, time would tell. She thought with pity of Maidie, first so angry and then so frightened. But the day had tired her out, and soon she, too, went to sleep, quieted by the familiar voice of the wind, and the come-and-go of Gus's breathing, close by her side.

The next morning nothing was said about either the fire or Maidie's going away. At breakfast everyone looked tired and Maidie was unusually silent. The children went off to school almost without speaking. Only Alvinia came back to give her father a quick hug.

"You were wonderful, Daddy," she said, and ran off embarrassed.

"Yes, you were!" Laura nodded, and he looked pleased at the praise, even though Maidie coughed disapprovingly.

When he had gone out into the barn the two women were left alone in the kitchen, but there was no tension between them. Maidie helped clear up the breakfast dishes, and talked about her childhood.

"I guess I got my own way too much after Pa died

93

and Ma went to work at the post office. I was only twelve and had to do everything at home. I just about reared Gus. My, what a cute little thing he was! People used to stop us on the street to admire him. For five or six years he was hardly out of my sight. I left school so I could take care of him, you know. I was a real little mother." She was silent and then said suddenly, "Turned out Gus was the only child I ever had. Maybe I got kind of set in my ways too young. I lost several good chances to marry because I wanted things as I wanted them and wouldn't bend."

"You must have been a very pretty girl," Laura said, pouring hot water from the kettle into the dishpan.

"Yes, I was, but a lot of good it did me," said Maidie somberly.

"Acted like a fool last night," she went on after a minute, drying dish after dish. "Didn't show proper good sense."

Once in a great while Maidie had these moments of self-criticism, but they never lasted. They always followed upon the heels of a particularly violent outburst of bad temper, which seemed for a few days to relieve some inner tension, but this then slowly began to build up again.

When Maidie went upstairs to make the beds in her room, Laura saw to the house plants. It was curious; when she was younger and happier she seemed to have no gift with flowers. Now that she no longer cared much what they did, they bloomed for her as they had never bloomed before.

"You work too hard," she told them silently. "All your relatives outside are resting, curled up in the darkness. They won't begin to stir until April."

When the plants were watered, she put on her sweater and took the paper bag in which she kept the garbage and went out. The snow had stopped falling sometime during the night and now lay on the ground soft as the inside of an egg shell. It was still cloudy overhead, but as she went through the door the sun appeared briefly, like a white eye glaring under a brow of black cloud. Then it was gone again. But the clouds were fraying into mist, and soon the blue sky would show through.

As she walked to the corner of the barn she was surprised to see rabbit tracks. No wild rabbit had ever come so close to the house and so far from the woods. Surely the Wabasso must have been here in the night! If so, she had been mistaken about yesterday's mysterious rabbit, or it was even possible that it had escaped its pursuer. She decided not to show Paul the tracks. For some time now he hadn't spoken of the Wabasso, since the day Gus said that he'd heard so much about that durned rabbit it was coming out of his ears.

Later in the morning she again went outdoors, to visit the beehive, neglected during so many storms. It stood under one of the apple trees in the shelter of the stone wall, facing southeast, as it had stood for twenty years. Nowadays the best honey came from the blueberry blossoms. Gus had taken the usual amount in the late summer, and Laura was a little worried because so many rainy days had followed during the season when the bees usually restocked their larder for their own use.

Now she was grieved to see the stand below the entrance of the hive piled with the brittle bodies of dead bees. Had they died of cold or of hunger, or of both?

In summer the doorway was about ten inches long and perhaps an inch and a half high, but the bees most often kept to the left side of their entrance, whose sill, after so many years of passage in and out, was a little worn, as the steps of an old house may be hollowed by constant use. In the fall a smooth piece of wood was inserted in the opening to keep the hive warmer in the cruel weather to come. This had a very small door cut into it, perhaps an inch wide, with a half-inch lintel, and through this winter entrance the dead bodies had been thrust.

Sorrowfully Laura took out the block. Inside, the floor of the hive was covered with dead bees.

"I suppose there were no bees left to carry them out," she thought.

She picked up a twig and swept away the corpses as well as she could. There were heaps caught in the corners of the hive. Altogether there must have been nearly a hundred dead bees, and there were probably others beyond the random reach of her little switch.

When she had cleaned the hive as well as she could, she put back the block to close the larger entrance again. She laid her ear against the white wood of the upper room but could hear no sound of humming.

"I wonder if the queen is still alive," she thought. "They would take care of her to the last."

But no, she thought, the hive was dead. One more relic from the past had gone back into the past; once more for her life had narrowed. She who had watched the paint peel, the fields run out, the blinds sag, the cattle go off in the butcher's truck, the machinery rust, said good-by once more. As she turned away, the hive looked like a headstone.

She did not mention the bees at lunch, which, like breakfast, was eaten very peacefully. Gus and Maidie talked quietly together, and now and then Laura said something in answer to a remark, usually from Gus, who seemed to want to include her in the conversation.

The sun, as though to celebrate this halcyon period, was now shining brightly, and close to the ground the snow was melting, so that the sagging surface had the look of a tufted white comforter.

After lunch Gus took the saw and went down into the beech grove to cut firewood. Laura wished that he would ask her to go along, but he didn't, and Maidie retired to her room for a nap as she felt one of her headaches coming on.

It would have been a good day to wash the kitchen windows and curtains, darkened by a winter of wood smoke, but Laura felt restless. She could not breathe in the house, the memory of the bees haunted her, and soon after the others had gone, she went out again.

It seemed much warmer than in the morning, and as she drew near the hive she saw bees buzzing about the entrance. In and out they crawled, some hanging upside down from the lintel, some coming right side up across the threshold. Once in the air, some flew off, and some clung to the sunny side of the hive, with a rapid pulsation of their wings, and others turned about and went back into the darkness almost at once.

The bodies of at least another dozen dead bees lay on the stand, but though she watched for a long time, no more were pushed out. Laura noticed that as those which had flown off returned, they stopped among the bodies and went from corpse to corpse, touching each. She could not help but read into their gestures an insect mourning and farewell.

Even as she stood there, the wind shifted a very little, and the sun passed into a white haze. It was enough for the bees. They felt the chill and retreated, leaving their dead piled on the tarpaper-covered stand.

"But some of you are alive!" Laura thought, rejoicing. "The swarm is weakened, but perhaps it will pull through."

In the darkness of the hive the remaining bees would cluster all through the cold weeks ahead. There was a chance, anyway, that when spring came some would be left to come out into the light. Laura had a sudden vision of many things coming out of the darkness into the light: bears and raccoons and wood-chucks from their caves and burrows, chipmunks looking about from the entrances of their holes, moths and insects crawling out from behind the loose folds of bark where they had hidden from winter, and everywhere, everywhere seeds and bulbs and buds struggling into the sun.

8

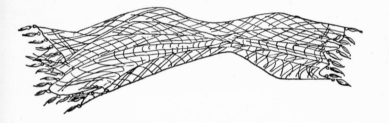

$\mathcal{T}$HE THAW which had brought out the bees, both living and dead, was of short duration, and the truce in the kitchen was equally short. With the next storm Maidie returned to her old resentments along with her shadow, Mildred, and Paul sank back into apathy. But Gus was changed. More and more often he turned to Laura, and he was less prone to ask for Maidie's advice or to take it when it was given, unasked. It may be, too, that Alvinia was less influenced by her older sister than she had been in those hours when she was not with her father. For years Laura had seen her own life as static, caught between a series of pressures under which her spirit was changing its shape. But now the pressures were shifting and she was freer. The change in Gus was often in her thoughts, and the knowledge that Little Joe was waiting in the valley for the call to High Farm, of which he was so sure, was an added strength to her, and sometimes she thought of Indian Joe, and at others found herself puzzling over the mystery of the Wabasso, or whatever rabbit it was which had taken shelter in Indian Joe's cabin.

Through February and the first weeks of March the storms continued. No one could remember such a winter. In the middle of March an ice storm brought down the electric and telephone wires on the hill, and after that the snow was too deep for the repair crews to venture up to High Farm. Laura brought the old oil lamps from the shelf in the shed where she kept them, and enjoyed seeing the softer light again, but Maidie was as indignant as though the heavens had planned their onslaughts with the set purpose of making her uncomfortable.

"And I can't telephone Ma!" she cried. "I don't know a thing about what's going on in town!"

But every winter, sooner or later, must give way to spring, and toward the end of March two or three days of sunshine seemed to herald the change of season.

One Saturday morning the sun rose bright and red out of the sea—too red, Laura thought—while all about her the worn bedroom glowed like the petals of a rose.

"Red sky at morning," she repeated almost to herself,

"Sailor, take warning.
Red sky at night,

Sailor's delight."

"A lot of those things never come true," said Gus, who had been lacing on his boots, taking her up, in the old, almost forgotten conversational way. "Looks like a good day."

He clumped off downstairs to light the first fire in the kitchen stove, but before brushing her hair Laura opened the top drawer of the chiffonier and took out her mother's Bible. She was teased by a half-memory and turning to the concordance found under "sky" what she wanted.

This was no time to be reading, and guiltily propping the book open with her mirror, she did up her hair, snatching a sentence at a time.

"When it is evening, ye say, It will be fair weather: for the sky is red.

"And in the morning, It will be foul weather to day: for the sky is red and lowring."

It might almost have been her father speaking, not Jesus! How near it made Galilee seem; two thousand years were folded up like a pocket handkerchief! But this was no time to be thinking of the Holy Land and weather saws, and with a final jab of a hairpin, she hurried off.

As it turned out, it was a very special day, for the far-off world in the valley once more interested itself in the affairs of High Hill, and soon after breakfast the snowplow grumbled up the lane, slicing its slow way through the snowbanks, and once more opened the road to the village.

As soon as she heard the throb of the big truck, Laura put a scarf over her head and went out to ask the men in for a cup of coffee from the pot which she had pushed over the fire.

Maidie tried to stop her.

"You can't ask a lot of men in here when Gus is in the barn. It isn't nice."

"I'm sure Gus won't mind. We've always given the snowplow crew coffee when they come after being up all night," Laura said, quickly slipping through the door into the lovely brightness of the outside world. She heard Maidie's voice still expostulating, but once more didn't listen, and only returned when she brought the men with her. As she led the way into the kitchen, there was Gus by the stove. Mildred had fetched him. The child was taking off her sweater, glancing smugly at her mother as she sat down beside Aunt Maidie. As usual, little Alvinia was standing close to her father, and Paul was nowhere to be seen.

Quietly Laura poured out the coffee while Maidie asked questions faster than they could be answered. Once everyone had coffee and doughnuts, Laura took up her darning. To see her no one would have guessed that she was bracing herself for the scene to follow, as soon as the last of the boots had clumped out of the kitchen and the door closed on the hasty visitors.

But after all there was no scene. Maidie acted as though the idea of refreshments had been her own.

"It makes them more willing to come," she said.

"And I'm so glad the road's open. Do you know what day tomorrow is?" Her face took on a coy expression. "It's my birthday. This year there won't be any crocuses on the plate, but at least I must have my cake."

Laura knew what that meant. For other birthdays any kind of cake would do, and candles from the bowl on the upper pantry shelf, and the old five-and-ten-cent-store rose-shaped holders, but Maidie must always have a Lady Baltimore cake and new surprise decorations.

"There aren't any figs or nuts," said Mildred, whose greed and thievishness flourished in safety under Aunt Maidie's protection.

"I know, darling. Mamma will drive down to town and get what she needs."

"No one goes out on these roads," Gus began, but Maidie interrupted sharply.

"Don't be silly, Gus. Laura can go as well as not. The plow's just been here. You don't have to worry about her. She can take care of herself."

"Well, be back as quick as you can." Gus gave in, though still a little uneasy. He opened the outside door and looked out. The clean sweet air flowed into the crowded kitchen.

"By golly, it *is* a fine day. Get on your duds, Alvinia. I'm going to put the wethers in the south pasture. There's a lot of bare ground there."

Laura said nothing, but she didn't approve. As for Maidie, she still thought that for sheep a little fresh air was the cure-all.

"First you'd better back the car out for her so she won't get herself stuck," said Maidie, referring to an incident which had taken place four winters earlier. Half an hour later, Laura was off, with her sister-in-law's last instructions sounding from the doorstep.

"Oh, and stop at Ma's and see how she is and tell her if she wants to send me a birthday present, I'd like the afghan that's on the foot of the sofa. And you might get some candy while you're about it."

Paul was still off somewhere by himself, Alvinia was with her father and old Rex, getting the wethers down to the south pasture, but Mildred showed last-minute signs of being willing to go to town, "just for the ride."

It was not part of Maidie's policy to encourage any of the children to be alone with Laura, who might, she felt, try to "influence" them.

"What would Auntie do all afternoon without her little girl?" she coaxed. "Poor Auntie's all alone! We'll have a little party, just you and me, while Mamma's away."

The word "party" was more than enough. The two looked at one another with the same look. A stranger would certainly have thought them mother and child, in feature and expression. Laura drove off alone, and at the sound of the passing car a small flock of juncos flew up out of the lilac bush where they had been sheltering.

She went slowly, against her will remembering the junco in the kitchen. On either side the rough road was banked high with recently plowed snow, hiding the stone walls and most of the bushes which had in recent years found footing beside them. Where the old crossroad at the shoulders of the lion climbed steeply down into the opposite valleys, she was surprised to find that the east branch had been cleared. No one lived on it now, except Rufe Dascomb in his tumbledown house, which he never left for months on end. She had expected to keep to the much longer main road, running north along the spine of the hill among the scattered farms.

Uncertain, Laura stopped the car and studied the sky. A haze had begun to whiten the blue and was ruffling into a hint of clouds along the horizon. Country-bred, she didn't like the look of it. She would have to hurry. The lesser risk was the narrow, deserted short cut, and this in the end she chose.

For the next miles Laura drove the old car with great care, edging her way over the rock slides and gullied ruts with the snow cliffs on either side almost touching the bumpers. Down she went past the deserted Seaton farm, past the Barlows' more recently closed house, with wooden boards nailed across all the lower windows, past the thin-blown smoke of Rufe Dascomb's, where only the kitchen ell was still habitable, and last of all past the Ellises', whose children had once been her friends, before they moved west and left the place to the owls and foxes. The East Road always made Laura feel sad. It was a ghost road, for she had known it when every house was filled with people, most of them now dead. The fields which they had tilled and the houses where they had lived were sadder than any graveyard.

On the level county road she was able to travel much faster. The day had lost its bloom; the gentian blue had gone out of the shadows, the sparkle from the snow. Now the sun shone in solemn silver, and the caw of an early crow or the distant hooting of a train came to Laura's ears more clearly than she would have wished.

"It's going to snow again," she thought. "I'll have to hurry."

And hurry she did. It was twelve miles to town, and when she got there, everything seemed to delay her. She wasted time finding a place to park; she had to wait for her turn in the stores; new ornaments for the cake were hard to find; friends and acquaintances stopped her on the street to ask how everyone was at High Farm. Now the sun looked like a quarter in a muslin pocket, and by the time Laura stopped at Mrs. Treadwell's house, a few flakes of snow were beginning to float about with a false air of uncertainty.

Mrs. Treadwell was a gentle old woman who always looked at her daughter-in-law with a faintly conspiratorial air, and there was an unspoken understanding in their kiss.

Today she was worried by the snow. She wanted Laura not to try to go home, but with the High Farm telephone out, the clamor that would be raised if

Laura didn't go back was more than she could face.

"Maidie would think I just wanted a nice long visit with you," Laura said affectionately, "and it's true I'd like nothing better. But I don't want them to be worried."

"Worried!" snorted Mrs. Treadwell. And to herself she added "Worried about her cake!" but she hurried off rather shakily to get the striped afghan which for thirty years she had pulled over herself every time she took a nap on the sofa.

"Now run along, dear, if you *have* to go! They say that a regular blizzard is on its way down from Canada. Worse than anything we've had."

Even in that short time, the snowflakes had dropped their fluttering pretenses and the sun had completely disappeared. Near by, it still seemed scarcely to be snowing, yet the distant air was white and houses and trees had taken on a shadowy and unsubstantial look.

Laura drove as fast as she dared. After the long winter even the black road was filled with honeypots and cracks, and the snow on either side had so narrowed it that it was necessary to slow down when meeting other cars. By now a northeast wind had come up, and a white dust of snow preceded her in eddies along the asphalt, confusing her eyes.

But the hint of danger exhilarated Laura. After all, the snow was a beautiful and open enemy. With quickened senses she rose to its challenge. All her daily life fell from her. It was a long, long while since she had felt so lighthearted.

If she took the main High Hill road she would never be very far from an inhabited house, but the chances of stalling the car would be greatly increased. She decided boldly to return as she had come, up the deserted East Road. By the time she had reached the turn, it was already too late to change her mind. She put the car in low and began to climb. Out of the shelter of the valley the wind was howling and the snow was drifting badly across the road. The flakes were coming faster and faster, in blinding eddies, and she never even knew when she passed Rufe Dascomb's.

Now by a wall she recognized an oak which marked the beginning of the Barlow place. A moment later, the storm suddenly let up and she had a clear view of the house.

"It isn't far to the turn," she thought, "and then the wind will be behind me." A rush of confidence flooded her. She was going to win after all, blizzard or no blizzard.

But the storm was only playing with her. It let her advance another fifty, seventy, a hundred feet. It let the old car plow through the first drift and the second and the third. But at the edge of their own land the fourth drift stopped it. She tried to put the power on easily, but even so the wheels began to spin. Laura found that she could go neither forward nor back. And now the storm threw itself upon High Hill in all its power, whirling and swirling about the stalled car, which stood out of sight of the farm, so that there was no chance, even if the air should clear again, of its being noticed.

"I'll just have to walk home," she thought. The way across the fields was only half as long as the way by the drifted road. Once more Laura made a choice. Carefully carrying the afghan and the box of chocolates, and putting the figs and walnut meats for Maidie's birthday cake in the pockets of her heavy coat, she slipped out in the lea of the car and stood for a moment to get her bearings.

9

$\mathcal{T}$HE BARRIER OF SNOW left by the plow was easier to climb than Laura had feared, and in the open and storm-swept field another surprise awaited her. The force of the wind had swept the loose snow away and laid bare the crust of the last thaw, and this held her weight. Although blinded and hustled, she was sure of her direction so long as she climbed upwards. The wind kept veering and eddying, but in general its force was at her back.

"I'll be home in no time," she thought, and the lift of relief showed how deep her uneasiness had been. But just as the thought took form in her mind, the crust broke through. One leg plunged down above the knee and she was thrown violently forward onto her outstretched hands, while the sharp edge of the snow sawed at her flesh. Shaken, she pulled herself upright again and regained her footing beyond the weak spot, but the same thing happened a few steps farther on. After the second fall, the crust no longer held her. Each step forward brought her almost waist-deep in the snow. The bottom of her coat was soon caked, and she began to flounder like someone caught in quicksand, at the same time deafened and bewildered by the howling of the wind.

"I wonder if the sheep are all right," she thought, on a slant of memory.

Once she shouted, "Help!" several times, but the shouting only tired her further, and she knew that her cries became a part of the crying wind. Who would be listening for her at High Farm? "She's stayed in town," Maidie would say. If Gus opened the door, Maidie would complain of the draft. Poor Rex was so deaf that he would hear nothing, and the children would accept what the grownups said without a second thought.

If Laura were to be saved, it must be by her own efforts. Resolutely she forced herself to go on. Now the sweat was running down her face, and freezing as it ran. Her muscles ached so that it seemed more than she could do to take another dreadful step. Blinded and deafened and exhausted, she struggled along, while all about her the snow swept by, running over the surface in eddies that confused her weary eyes.

"If only Papa were still at the farm," she thought. She could imagine her mother saying anxiously, "Will, do you suppose Laura could have been stuck on the road?" And her father would have said, "I'll just walk down a ways and make sure." "I'll stand in the door and ring the dinner bell so you'll know where you are," her mother would have added. More than once she had so stood, in hood and coat and mittens, ringing and ringing the big bell to bring one of them home through a storm, home to warmth and to love!

Just then something went by, almost hidden in the blowing snow. It was so white that she clearly saw only the gray patches at the tip of its ears and a dark shining eye. It was a snowshoe rabbit, seeking shelter from the storm, hopping along slowly, as though, like her, it were exhausted. The sight of anything alive encouraged her, and then she thought, "A wild animal will know where to go," and stumbled after it. But suppose this was the Wabasso? He seemed to have few instincts, less perhaps than she had herself. She paused doubtfully, and the rabbit, too, paused. "At least," she thought, "it's alive," and again she struggled after it, sometimes on her hands and knees.

Now the largest drift of all was in front of her. Laura crawled over it, impeded by her coat and the afghan she carried over her sholders, her body sinking deeply into the snow's furry softness. Unable to see where she was going, she all at once pitched forward into calmness and rest. The rabbit had disappeared, but at the time in her relief she scarcely noticed that it was gone. She could see again, breathe again, think and feel again, while the blizzard sailed by in its white rage over her head.

"What has happened?" she thought, filled with wonder. "Where am I?" And then she knew that she must be in the lea of the great stone wall which divided the hayfield from the old barley field. Bushes and brambles and a few young pines added to the windbreak. The snowdrift came over them all in a wave, bowing down the branches, but here where she crouched like a hare there was very little snow and no wind at all. Here for a little while she was safe to rest and gather her strength for the longer, steeper, more terrible field ahead, which lay between her and the house.

Long ago, in one of her falls she had lost the box of candy, but the afghan was still with her, and now she shook the snow from it and laid it on the ground against the wall and crawled under the hedge's low roof of snow-covered branches.

From somewhere far off came a memory of stories that she had heard. This safety, this warmth, this relaxation could be dangerous, too. Whatever happened, she must not go to sleep, or she might never wake up. Whatever happened, she must not go to sleep. Go to sleep. Sleep.

It was probably some hours later when she woke. Darkness had come, and it was very quiet. At first she did not remember where she was, and only slowly the horror of the storm came back to her.

"I haven't frozen, after all," she thought. "Perhaps

I had better stay here until morning. By then the blizzard may have blown itself out. It looks as if a rabbit has saved my life again."

It was so silent that after a while she began to wonder if the storm might not be over already. Last night there had been a new moon, with the old moon in its arms, always a sign of storm, if anyone had stopped to think of it. She decided that she would crawl a little way beyond her shelter and see if it were still snowing. If not, she might even see the lighted windows of the house, and be able to go on with them to guide her.

Full of hope, Laura started away from the stone wall, but where there had been open space beyond the bending branches, there was now a solid snowbank, so that she found herself a prisoner in a narrow tunnel running along the wall. She knew that sometimes partridges were caught like this under low hemlock boughs where they had taken shelter and later on were found, starved to death. But she was not a partridge. Surely a woman could dig her way out!

Calmly enough, Laura tried to loosen the tips of the branches from the bank in which they were embedded, but they were tightly held, and her efforts only brought masses of snow down upon her from above, half smothering her. Exhausted as she was, she dared not risk anything more. Inching her way cautiously along the wall, she reached a clearer space where the roof of snow had not been disturbed, and to this she dragged the afghan, shook it bit by bit, and again wrapped it about her.

It was not cold under the snow, and when the first terror of finding herself a prisoner had died down, she began to take stock of her situation.

"If it's a short storm, I may be all right," she thought. "If it's a long one, I suppose I shall die here. I wish I hadn't lost the box of candy."

Only later she remembered the figs and walnut meats in her pockets and ate her first small meal, which gave her renewed courage. In a house of snow, thirst was no problem.

"It's only death, after all," she thought. "Everyone dies some time or other."

But she was not always so fatalistic. As the hours went by, sometimes she felt recurrent horror at the idea of being buried alive and dying so strangely.

"If only I could see the sky again!" she thought. "It's horrible not even knowing if it's day or night." But with time she grew more accustomed to her prison. And when she woke, perhaps on the second day, she found that, after all, there was light, a glowing blue light, lovely though faint. She could see nothing by it but the darkness of her own body like a shadowy bee in a blue morning-glory, but this return to sight was a great pleasure to her, partly because it surrounded her with beauty and partly because it showed her that far above her roof of snow the sun must be shining, and if the sun shone, people would begin to stir, and sooner or later her disappearance would be discovered. Not that she felt any certainty that the discovery would come soon enough to save her, but at least she felt less deeply buried alive in darkness.

After the light came, she had more courage and began to sing hymns to herself, buzzing away very much like a bee, she thought. The familiar verses quieted her mind, lulling her back into her childhood when everything had seemed so secure. She was not a good singer, her voice was unsure, but in the old days she had enjoyed singing as she worked, until one day, soon after Maidie came, she had turned from the ironing board and found her sister-in-law shaking with silent laughter.

"Oh, go on!" Maidie cried. "I love to hear you! I just happened to think of a joke someone told me."

But Laura had not gone on, either then or later. Here in her cell of snow she could. There were no ears, certainly, to hear her, and the singing comforted her more than prayers, for after all she was prepared to live or to die, and her prayers were little more than "Thy will be done."

"How peaceful it is!" she thought. "There is nothing I need do but sit here and think quietly of whatever I want to. Even though I can't see it, I know that I am in a white room, like a doctor's waiting room, waiting for someone to open the door." If it were Death whose hand was on the doorknob, he would come in very softly. There was nothing for her to be afraid of. Why had she been afraid?

"We are all afraid of words," she thought. " 'Exhaustion,' 'starvation,' 'smothering,' 'frozen,' 'in sight of her own home.' They are all frightening ideas. And yet they aren't true. Here am I like a bulb safe in the darkness of the earth, or the bees in their hive, or the rabbit that lives in Indian Joe's cabin."

She had only to think of Indian Joe to feel comforted. She hoped that she had some of the same blood in her veins.

"I can't perform any of his magic," she thought. "No wind shakes this white room of mine, and no voices of spirit animals will keep me company. But at least I can try to take everything calmly, as he did." And she thought of Indian Joe's death, under the worn rabbit robe, more skin than fur, and of what he said to his little grandson: "You'll come back. You and me."

Perhaps he had tried to come back. Perhaps he had . . . Suddenly something logical in her mind said, "But if that *was* Indian Joe, he led you into this trap. He betrayed you when you followed him."

Perhaps he knew best. Perhaps it was better for her to die. But because she had begun in the last weeks to hope again, she wanted to live. She schooled herself once more to patience. She accepted the idea of death, and she must make the most of this quiet waiting in Death's anteroom.

"Suppose," she thought on another day or during another night, "that I shouldn't die, but should rise like Lazarus."

And she began to wonder about Lazarus. Had he

124

been glad to be recalled to life? Or had he been sorry? And what difference would the fact that he had been dead make in him? Surely he would not live on just as he had lived before! Would he demand more or less of life? Be gentler, or perhaps harsher? Did he become a saint, or perhaps a madman? Of one thing Laura felt certain: he would not be the same.

Often she remembered her childhood, so solitary and so happy, with all the beauty of the world stretched at her feet and the house filled with love. "No person can live alone," she thought. A woman is like a tree, and her relationships to others are the roots which support her, so that she may come to leaf and flower and fruit. An unhappy person may still be useful, but only happiness can give happiness.

Looking back, Laura could see that the first year of her marriage *had* been happy. She missed her father, but her mother was still there, mistress of the farm, and Gus had seemed to fit so well into the High Hill ways. He had loved the farm in those days. A baby was coming. How she had looked forward to that baby, and Gus had been as pleased as she was.

Thank goodness, her mother had not been cheated of holding her first grandchild in her arms! But only a month later she had suffered a heart attack, and after the funeral, Maidie had suggested coming up to High Farm for a few weeks to help Laura. Laura remembered how grateful she had felt. And at first Maidie did help, if not a great deal, at least a little, and during that autumn she had pretended to like the farm and life on High Hill. But by the next spring, Maidie had laid aside the pretext of helping and of liking her surroundings.

Not quite understanding what was happening, Laura had watched Maidie take control as though the farm were hers. Her complete inexperience never kept her from giving Gus advice on every detail of his work, nor him from taking it.

Her own suggestions, born of a lifelong familiarity with the farm, were brushed aside with increasing impatience, as though they were criticisms, and the worse things went, the greater was his impatience. Soon she stopped giving advice, or spoke with hesitating apologies.

Yet life didn't change all at once. At first there were long periods of happiness for Laura, when Gus still seemed very close to her. But as the years went by, these periods grew shorter and more infrequent, while very gradually Maidie edged between them. As for Mildred, Maidie had made the child into an image of herself. If Laura tried to direct or check her, it was "Come to Auntie! Mamma doesn't understand little girls the way Auntie does!" So it had been with all three children, though Mildred remained Maidie's pet, her love, her little dolly. Paul shook everyone off and went his own way. While he had the Wabasso things had been better, but now they were bad again, and his teacher was writing home about his schoolwork, and Gus scolded him a dozen times a day.

Alvinia would be all right. She had plenty of git-up-

and-git of her own, which sometimes reminded Laura of her own father. And she loved and was loved. Although she was so little, she had no more need of Laura than did the others.

"If I die," Laura thought, slowly eating the meats of two nuts, "Maidie will say it served me right for letting in the junco, and if she has her way, they'll sell High Farm. But I don't think Gus will want to, and I think he'll miss me. I don't want to die, either, especially now, when we're just beginning to get back to each other."

It was not that she was afraid. Let Death come when he willed. But she would prefer to live, even the life she knew so well. Again a familiar image came to her. Somewhere the trees were spreading out their bare branches into the air. Now that the leaves were gone, they looked like roots, but since air is more fluid than earth, the boughs were longer and more poised than roots. But their greed was the same, drawing from sun and air as the roots drew from earth and the underground springs.

So Laura, too, drew her sustenance from everything about her, from every season, from distant mountains and far-off sea, from lake and rock and the wind and her own thoughts. She was learning not to look back at old frustrations and sorrows, nor ahead to new ones. Now she lived in the minute, taking a quick, small joy in the smell of baking, the shadow of a bird, the bark of a fox in the spring woods. If she, like Lazarus, were to rise from the dead, even if after all

she and Gus could never find one another as she had
begun to hope they might, still, even so, once more
the lilac would open its leaves and once more the
catbird would sit on her eggs among its branches

10

$\mathcal{H}$OURS LATER, Laura woke up, thinking, "I am getting weaker and there are only a few nuts left." She thought of her father and mother and of her father's people, who lay in the graveyard, and of Indian Joe and his wife Abbie, whose bodies rested beside theirs. They all seemed as much alive now to her as did the living people, moving about the kitchen at High Farm, not very far from where she crouched, buried, yet not quite dead. The living people did not belong to her, kindly and simply, as the dead did. Yet she thought of them one by one, lovingly and sadly, taking her farewell of each: of Gus, her husband, who was forever a part of her, of Mildred with her dissatisfied face in its bright hair, of Paul's blind look, and of Alvinia, who was the only truly happy person in the family, and last of Maidie, who seemed to her like the lilac at the door, something which had been meant to flower, but which had been twisted out of its natural shape. Yet each of them loved and was loved—even Paul had had the Wabasso, and having loved once, might love again.

"Something was wrong with me," Laura thought. "They could love each other but not me. If there were just one of them who really loved me, I would find my way back somehow. Love is a road, and I have lost it."

Something was wrong with her. Her tired mind picked the word up. It had begun with Maidie, yes, but it takes two to make a quarrel. Yet she had never quarrelled. It takes two to make a situation, then. She had never rebelled, never stood up for herself. Could it be that sometimes it may be wrong to turn the other cheek? That the one who is slapped is only the other half of the one who slaps? And equally to blame? What support could the children turn to in her, beyond the physical food and warmth and clothing she had given them? Working for them all day, had she not just as surely deserted them? And Gus! She had let their happiness slip away without fighting for it! Was there a connection between his recent tendency to cut loose from Maidie's apron strings and those times when she herself had shut her ears to Maidie's commands? Had he unconsciously been waiting for her encouragement to rebel against the influence wielded over him from earliest childhood? Had they begun to find the way back to each other, stumblingly and blindly?

"One can be too patient," she thought. "By putting up with so much bossing, I gave them all into Maidie's hands. Yes, and I finished Maidie's ruin, too. She might have been very different now if I had not egged her on by always giving in to her. Too much of a good thing can be a bad thing. Why, Maidie's bossiness was fine when she was twelve and such a responsible little girl! We've both of us run to seed in these last years. I'm as much to blame as anyone," she repeated. "I see now what I should do, if only I could live to do it."

She must have drowsed after that. When she woke up the cave was blue again, and she was aware of a slight sound, like a gnawing, she thought at first, and a vision of rabbits crossed her mind. But as she listened more closely, she realized that what she heard was a trickle of water among the stones behind her, and, reaching out, she found that the ground near her was damp. The snow of her prison, too, seemed more packed and crystallized, old snow which had lost its white fur softness. How long had this been going on? Several times, using great caution, she had tried to burrow out of her hole, but each time the snow had fallen into her excavation and she had given up her attempts at escape.

Now when she might be able to succeed, she no longer had the strength. Her thoughts came slowly and confusedly, but she forced them to steady; and after a time she began to feel along the ground until she found a stick, not too brittle, she hoped, for her purpose. She remembered that she had on a red rayon scarf, and this she now tied carefully to the end of the stick, and began to push it up through the snow above her head. Her first attempt failed, and her second and third. Sometimes the branches above her were too thick, or the stick was rotten and broke, or the scarf caught on something and came off. But she did not give up. Moving slowly and obstinately along her burrow, she carefully worried off a straight, live branch from above her and finally succeeded in forcing it through the tangle of bushes and the eaves of snow overhead. Trembling with the effort, she felt it break through the last crust and come out far above her in the open, pressureless air.

"Is the scarf still on it?" she wondered, but could do nothing to find out, for if she pulled the stick back, the scarf would certainly come off.

"I've done what I can," she thought and drowsed again, and dreamed that she was trying to call for help but could make no sound, although her life depended on it. White rabbits were in the dream somewhere, whether trying to help her or to smother her she couldn't tell, but they were pressing close about her and she was trying to break through them, when she awoke to a new nightmare of falling snow against which she fought weakly, smothering now in earnest.

But not for long.

Hands from above fumbled and caught her. She was being pulled up into the blinding light and air. She heard voices, a voice.

"Gus!" she cried. Her husband had come to save her.

But it was not Gus. It was Paul in his old reefer and red and black checked cap, deep in the drift, his snowshoes standing upright behind him in the untrampled snow. And he was crying and kissing her, saying "Mamma" over and over again as if he couldn't stop.

"I have risen like Lazarus," she thought, "and see with new eyes."

Above them shone the all too violent blue of the sky. Under them lay the snow, wrinkled like a winter apple. And beyond stood High Farm with the smoke rising straight up into the air from the kitchen chimney.

"Where's Daddy?" she asked.

The boy answered something about Daddy's being in town, but Laura could not understand what he meant. She was so weak she had to concentrate all her will on keeping upright while Paul fastened the snowshoes on her numbed feet. It was a hard climb up to the farm for them both, but, dizzy and blinking and stumbling though her body might be, her spirit was filled with joy, and Paul's eyes were bright and clear as they had been when he was a little boy. Rising from the dead, she had found her son, a new son, as she would find Gus and the others, new as she herself was newborn into life.

"How did you know where to look for me, Paul?" she asked once as they rested, panting, and he said,

"I was looking for something else. I didn't know that I'd find you. We all thought you'd stayed with Grandma. Aunt Maidie was sure of it. She said you were enjoying yourself while she did all the work!"

Yes, of course. Laura had never thought of that. Maidie must have been very busy, while for once Laura had sat and taken her ease in the white room. She smiled a little to herself.

"I think I can go on now," she said. "What a help you are, Paul! I could never make it alone."

Someone must have seen them from a window, for as they staggered up to the shed door, it flew open and Alvinia ran out and braced her small body against her mother's, across from Paul.

"What's happened, Mamma? Are you all right?" she asked, supporting her toward the door and then bending down to the slow task of undoing the old cracked straps of the snowshoe nearest her, while Paul worked on the other.

Maidie and Mildred now appeared, Maidie asking sharply, "Where did you leave the car?" Apparently she thought that Matt Armstrong had driven the plow up as far as the crossroads and that Laura had followed in her car from the village and by some coincidence had happened to meet Paul. Could she really have believed it, seeing Laura so haggard and dishevelled? Probably. Maidie could believe anything she had set her mind on, sweeping aside all contradictory evidence, even of her own senses, and now worry and housework had accelerated her natural irritability.

"It's a pity you couldn't get home before this!" she went on. "Leaving me to do everything!"

"I did a lot!" Mildred reminded her with equal irritability.

Under the children's excited hands the buckles were slow to open, and Laura reached out to support herself against the door frame, facing her sister-in-law.

"Let's make a new beginning, Maidie," she said, speaking slowly and evenly. "Let's be friends." If Maidie had ever been aware of other people, she would have known that something had changed. If she had been sensitive, she would have been warned in time.

But Maidie had a headache—real, for once—and she was blind to what was happening before her eyes. Here was Laura back from her junketings, trying to soft-soap her, and Maidie would have none of it. And why hadn't she told them how Gus was?

"Friends," Maidie mimicked. "When it's all because of you that my brother's been half killed!"

"Gus! Half killed!" Laura cried, swaying where she stood.

Paul straightened up and glared at his aunt.

"That's not true, Aunt Maidie, and you know it. Daddy's only got a broken leg. And he went to bring in the sheep. He wasn't hunting for Mamma. He thought she was in town!"

"It doesn't matter. If he hadn't married her, he wouldn't have been hurt."

Maidie saw the tears running down Laura's cheeks, and the sight seemed to goad her on.

"I blame myself, too," she said, speaking slowly and clearly. "If I hadn't been such a fool as to pick you out for him to marry, it would never have happened." All the bitterness of a bitter spirit gathered itself into a final thrust. "There were several girls he preferred at the time, but I insisted. So I am partly to blame."

And now a woman she had never seen looked back at Maidie. The stranger said, "You have accepted the blame, so there is nothing more to say. Paul, Alvinia, help me in."

Maidie, and with her Mildred, both looking a little bewildered, fell back from the door, and Laura, helped by the younger children, stumbled into the untidy kitchen and sat down in Maidie's chair in the warm corner, while Mother Brindle, for once unnoticed, turned about her ankles.

By now Laura could scarcely speak, but there was something she had to know before she could rest.

"Tell me about Daddy," she said, looking at Paul.

"He went out with me and Rex to bring in the wethers," the boy told her. "It was snowing so hard we couldn't see three feet ahead, and old Rex led Daddy out onto a ledge of snow over the south cliff. It held Rex, but Daddy was too heavy. They both went over. I was just behind. I got down to them by the cliff path, but Rex was dead and Daddy had broken his left leg above the ankle."

"Then the snowplow came and the men brought Daddy back and took him to the doctor. Poor Daddy!" Alvinia was crying, leaning against her mother's knee.

"They brought in the sheep, too," Paul went on. "They were all right. And, Mamma, it was queer about Daddy. He didn't seem upset. He seemed almost glad it had happened. 'After this I'll need help for a while,' he said. 'No one could expect a lame man to handle this big place alone.' He said he was going to send word to that Indian who was up here this winter."

"Daddy's brave," Alvinia said proudly, her tears beginning to dry. "And you're brave, too, Mamma. Where did Paul find you? What happened to you, darling Mamma?"

At the moment Laura could only give Alvinia a hug. She had not the strength to answer. And all her thoughts were of Gus. Dear Gus! Now she realized how great a pride had kept him fighting the unequal battle, as lonely in his way as she had been in hers. He had wanted to prove himself, to Maidie, who had dominated him, but more to her, his wife, and most of all to himself. With stubborn courage he had piled the odds too heavily against himself, but now at last he could accept help. Dear Gus! Now they would have each other, and neither need stand alone any more. What Maidie had said was not important, even if it were true. They had once been happy together and would be again. Without Maidie to stir up trouble.

Paul, usually so silent, was talking on:

"Matt had been on the road since the beginning of the storm, so he didn't know if you were at Grandma's. Daddy asked."

"How long ago was that?"

"Four days."

"I was buried for four days," she thought.

In the warmth her mind was growing clearer, and she seemed to come into a second strength. Quietly she turned to Maidie, who was standing by the sink watching her sharply. By now the older woman must have understood that Laura had been caught by the storm on her way home, but probably she thought that she had stayed in the car or taken shelter in one of the empty houses, and at this late date she scarcely knew how to ask.

"The storm's over." Laura spoke with that new air of authority. "Matt will try to get back as soon as he can to bring word of Gus. I'm sure the men will be willing to dig out the car so we can get to town to see him. And when we go, Maidie, have your things packed. You won't come back here."

Maidie was startled.

"I've lived here for thirteen years, and now you turn me out like a dog," she began shrilly.

"Yes."

"If Aunt Maidie goes, I'm going with her!" cried Mildred, throwing her arms about her aunt's waist. The last days had shown the child a new and less

140

attractive side of Aunt Maidie, but the long loyalty still held.

Laura was unmoved. It was to have this strength, this assurance, that for four days she had been buried between life and death.

"All right, Mildred. I think you'll be happier in town, for a while at least. But you must talk it over with Daddy. And of course this is your home, always, whenever you want to come back."

"I'll go down to see Daddy, but I want to stay here at the farm with you," Alvinia chimed in, and Laura smiled at her and nodded.

But Maidie and Mildred stared at her in silence. What had happened to Mamma, who had always been so loving and so quick to give in?

They were frightened.

"You're excited," said Maidie. "You don't know what you're saying. What do you suppose people will think if you turn out your own daughter, let alone me? You need a rest, Laura dear, and a nice hot cup of tea."

Her manner had become conciliatory. She almost ran to the stove to push the kettle over the fire.

"It's too late," said Laura. "I'm not the same person, Maidie. Like Lazarus, I have risen from the dead. I don't care a button what people say. I'm sorry for you, Maidie, but you can't stay." And to herself she added, "For your own sake, as well as for ours."

The exhaustion which she had held back was returning. Soon she could rest. She was almost through.

"And what about you, Paul? Will you stay here or go down to the village?"

"Do you think I'd leave you for Aunt Maidie?" the boy almost shouted at her. "I used to be so confused I didn't know what to think. She made fun of you all the time behind your back. And Daddy . . . well, I wanted him to like me. And you didn't stand up for yourself. I didn't know what to think. But when you didn't come home, and Aunt Maidie kept saying you were having a high old time in town while she did all your work, when I knew she was the one who had sent you—"

"You're a wicked, ungrateful boy after all I've done for you!" broke in Maidie furiously.

But Paul never turned his eyes from his mother's.

"Then last night it was the strangest thing. I dreamed that the Wabasso was caught in a snare by the stone wall of the old barley field. In my dream it was fall, with the blueberry bushes turning red and there wasn't any snow at all, and I heard him screaming and screaming. When I woke up it was just as real as when I dreamed it. I couldn't wait to go out and look. Aunt Maidie said it was all nonsense, but I went anyway. And there was your red scarf like a flag in the snow."

So the Wabasso really had saved her again, this time by a dream! Laura could doubt no longer who the Wabasso was. "You will come back, Little Joe. You and me." And they had come back. Little Joe would come and help Gus and bring back the luck of High Farm. But it was his grandfather who had saved her and who had led her to the gate of death, so that she might learn to face herself and to make the life he had saved worth living. When she was stronger she would tell Paul, but this was not the moment.

Mother Brindle, ignored so long, leaped into Laura's lap and mewed, looking up into her face.

"You miss poor Rex," Laura said. "I miss him, too." With an effort, she raised her hand and patted the cat's thrusting head. "Now lift her off, Paul, and help me upstairs. I've got to lie down."

"Help your mother," Maidie whispered, giving Mildred a push toward Laura, but Mildred hung back, and Laura got to her feet with Paul's arm about her while Alvinia boosted valiantly.

Together they slowly left the kitchen and slowly climbed the narrow stairs, Laura dragging herself upwards along the rail. The two in the kitchen stood listening to the footsteps overhead. Then they heard the bed creak as Laura lay down. There was a pause. Paul and Alvinia must be helping her off with her shoes and drawing the comforters over her.

If they spoke, the others below heard only a murmur. Then came Paul's quick steps, followed by a voice calling after him.

"Just bread and cheese. And make the tea good and strong!" said the voice. It was not the words, but the tone which shook the listeners by the stove.

"Can that be her?" thought one.

"Can that be Mamma?" thought the other.

And then the door closed and Paul came whistling down the stairs.

Date Due